DAY
LABORERS

DIANE TAYLOR

ISBN 978-1-957220-52-9 (paperback)
ISBN 978-1-957220-53-6 (digital)

Rushmore Press LLC
1 800 460 9188
www.rushmorepress.com

Printed in the United States of America

It was a sunny day in May, and Spring in New York had finally come. People were crowding the streets shopping, visiting and enjoying outdoor activities again. Also it was moving day for Carmen and Venito. After being together for more than a year they had agreed to move in together. May is always a better month in New York for moving. It was Memorial Day weekend and they had decided to move to their own apartment across the street from Yankee Stadium, which is located in the Bronx. Venito and his Popps (his dad) were baseball men and they were part owners of the team. It was important that they maintain a good working relationship with the players, managers, owners and investors. So Venito felt it necessary to be within walking distance to the stadium. Months before the move Carmen and Venito were window shopping getting ideas what they needed for their apartment. Venito had always lived in the brown stone that his sister Margaret and husband Nicky owned after his father Freddie sold it to them and moved to Bethpage in the Long Island region. The brown stone was located in Brooklyn on Moffat Street, known for multi family homes. Venito rented space in the basement of the building and used the space just to sleep their on occasions. Venito did a lot of walking as many New Yorkers do. One of Venito's stores was located within blocks of his apartment. He owned four Office Supply stores. The other three located in Harlem on 125th Street, SoHo Chinatown store was off of Chambers Street in Low Manhattan East Side and Midtown Manhattan on 34th and Fifth Avenue. Close to Macy's Herald Square. Venito had only brought Carmen to his apartment their three times. Of course his sister had invited her to dinner one of the times, because she was Mary's third grade teacher and Mary was quite fond of her. Mary was Margaret and Nicky's daughter, they also had a three year old son, named Zack, short for Zachariah. For the most part Venito's apartment was a big room with a half bath, sectioned off with partition separating the storage area that Margaret used to house unwanted and unused items. There was nothing for Venito to move from there but clothes and personal items. Therefore everything for he and Carmen's new apartment needed to be purchased. Carmen had always lived with Momma Rosa her whole life and never bought items for a place. For as long as she can remember Momma Rosa lived in Hell's Kitchen in a two bedroom apartment. And as far back as Carmen remembers, Momma Rosa did not change things around that much. Before the winter had left during the Christmas holidays they were looking at furniture and items for their move in the Spring. One of Carmen's most prized items for the apartment that they found was in an antique shop several blocks from their new apartment, it was a dining room table with carvings of a Mexican migration of immigrants and celebration symbols. The table was made of solid mahogany wood, it seated up to six and provided the table leaflet would seat eight people. Momma Rosa helped Carmen understand her Mexican heritage every since she was old enough to speak. The history of the wood carvings described some of the activities that were carved into the table. Carmen also did a term paper in the 8th grade history class on her Mexican history. So therefore she wanted this table so bad and she didn't care about how expensive it was, she wanted it. Venito was in the habit of buying her whatever she wanted and did not hesitate when she asked for it.

The two of them took it out of layaway and decided to carry it home. Carmen was so excited that finally it was theirs, that she jumped on Venito with her legs wrapped around his waist and arms around his neck, pulling him tight to her bosom kissing his face and crying tears of joy. As they began to walk down the street with the table, Venito would walk backwards and sideways, the heaviest part leaning on him and Carmen would always be facing forward. People gave way to them on the sidewalk as they approached them and some people even commented about how nice of a table it was and how lucky they were to find one so close to their apartment without worrying about the delivery fee. Delivery fees can be quite pricey in New York and no one hardly sells you any things without imposing a delivery charge. Most of the stores have to use independent delivery services. Of course because of how heavy the table was, they had to put it down several times to rest before reaching their apartment. Once they arrived at the apartment, Venito was concerned about Carmen going up to their second floor apartment carrying her end of the table. Luckily Venito saw two teenaged boys who he called over and offered them money to help him carry the table up to their place.

Hell's Kitchen was called Hell's Kitchen because it was viewed as being the lowest and filfthest neighborhood in the city. The community located between 8th Avenue to the Hudson River North and South from 34th Street to 59th Street, near the Port Authority, bus station and stretched down to Central Park. In the mid 1850's is was predominately Irish immigrants, who escaped the Famine back in Ireland. Although there were pockets of German, Italians and Jewish immigrants Jewish immigrants mostly working from the docks West Side, known for gruesome murder and riots in 1881, hence the name was given to the neighborhood by a Journalist who describe the area as Hell's Kitchen and the name stuck. It was a pretty tough neighborhood as the elements of Hell's Kitchen constantly consisted of various criminal gangs, that took over control of import goods, illegally unloading cargo ships and tried taking over labor unions. In addition, seize control over the railroads. The groups moved on up to Harlelm to occupy the Cotton Club. Venito Frederico Marnoonase was born in Palermo, Sicily, June 15, 1978 to Frederico Venito Marnoonase and Remona. That is what he was told and his birth Certificate says the same. However, the truth of the matter is that his mother did not die in child birth, but his father had his real mother put away in mental institution. His sister Margaret Denise Manoonase was three years old and Venito was one year old when their father and Aunt Josephine (who posed as Frederico's wife in actuality, she was Frederico's sister), brought them from Sicily and were made American citizens. They were sponsored here by Frederico's older brother Peter. Once here, Aunt Josephine changed her name and was married later to an Irishman. Venito had always known her as his Aunt and did not know that she entered America as his mother. She was also the one who raised him and his sister. Frederico did not marry again until some years later. He only did this to seem normal. Venito's Uncle Peter was already involved in mob activities and got his father into it, it became known as the family business. Growing up in New York Venito never questioned his father about anything about his late night activities because he was in bed by the time his father met for meetings as well as not knowing his activities early in the morning. All he know is that his father owned a couple of laundry mats, several grocery stores an apartment building and that he also worked with Uncle Peter. Some of the business were co-owned by several other people, not always Italians. While in school Venito went to school in Brooklyn and his father owned a deli/grocery store a few blocks from where he lived. Venito's stepmother did not have to worry about fixing him and Margaret breakfast because they would leave their house early enough to go by the deli and get some breakfast, also their lunchboxes were kept there. So they pickup their lunchboxes every school day and drop back off to be refilled and were left over the weekend. Their step mother's name was Sarah, they called her mom. Venito periodically would get in fights with the school kids for one thing or another. Margaret was a beautiful blonde headed girl who stood tall, crooked teeth, but a beautiful smile. Because they had to wear uniforms she did not have many ordinary clothes, accept when they went to Mass and regular church services she wore dresses. Good Catholic girls dressed modestly and were taught to act like a lady. She sang in the children's choir and participated in various church activities. Venito was an alter boy they helped the priest during Mass as well as other specialty services. Just like teenage boys his age they chased after girls. One time some neighborhood boys cornered a girl visiting their neighborhood from Maryland, staying for the summer with her grandmother. She was somewhat unattractive and talked funny, a slight southern accent, she went to the store for her grandmother one day, however she did not make it back in the allotted time that her grandmother had given her, so she sent some other kids to look for her only to find her screaming and crying, clothes torn and she was bleeding from her vaginal. Some of the boys who Venito hung around with had raped her and ran away. At that time, Venito was with them, but did not take part in raping her, and did not try to stop the three boys who took turns with her. However, once it was known who all the boys were that were involved, Venito was also charged and all seven boys were sentenced to a Juvenile Detention Center. Some had a lesser charge, Venito, along with Stanley Newman spent only six months there due to their father's being well known in the community as well as knowing the judge and the prosecutors. They were released and their record was expunged. Venito lived a pretty good life, that afforded him with money always in his pocket, nice clothes. One day at the dinner table, Carmen asked her grandmother where was she born and to tell her about her father, who was Mexican. Your father, Javier was my only child, that survived. I followed my boyfriend from Mexico, we crossed over the Mexican boarder near Juarez and entered a small town know for taking in Mexicans who had no papers and were considered illegal. Not long after being in the U.S. my then boyfriend found out I was pregnant with Javier, his name was Jesus. We lived in a one room shack. Most of the housing there were considered unlivable. It was an old military camp, but was occupied by Mexicans and others who want a better opportunity to make a life for them and their families. The work was found on a daily basis. Most migrant workers were hired and paid the same day. There were no guarantee that you would have work each day. I did whatever I could do with Javier by my side while his dad brought most of his daily earnings to me.

One day he did not come home and I didn't know what happened to him. So the next day one of the guys who worked with him gave me an envelope like the one that had money in it and a note was with it too. Jesus had gotten on a migrate bus taking workers to California to work and he said that he was sorry. So Javier and I stuck it out until I could get enough money to go to New York. The nuns and priest at the church there gave me some people to contact when I got to New York. It took up to five days to get here. We had to stop in Chicago and get a hotel room because we both got sick. After a one night stay, we continued on our journey. We got this place in Hell's Kitchen and had been here every since. Of course I married a Puerto Rican from my job, we were pregnant with twins and I fell going up to our apartment and lost the babies. We didn't try again, a few years later he got burned on the job, a boiler exploded and he was killed. So Javier and I were on our on once again. Carmen was eight years old and knew that she was born in New York on August 21, 1992, but she knew little of her mother and her mother's family.

Momma Rosa spoke little English and always communicated in Spanish. Momma Rosa told Carmen that she began with her receiving her from a Socialworker who picked her up from John F. Kennedy Airport, when she was almost a year old. Her mother had abandoned her in Puerto Rico, leaving her with her grandmother who could not take care of her and asked if her Grandmother in the states would care for her. She did not want to see you go into the Foster Care System. Momma Rosa asked Javier, Carmen's father if he would have any objections to you living with her. He replied that that would be a great idea, but also it maybe a little challenging, due to the fact that he had been an adult for sometime and that maybe she was getting to old to deal with a baby. Momma Rosa was more than thrilled to have someone in her life that was related to her, since Javier was her only family in New York, but was incarcerated. When the Socialworker knocked on her door with Carmen, Momma

Rosa, almost cried. The baby looked like her mother and Javier. She knew right away that Carmen was Javier's child. She noticed her eyes a charcoal color, round face with orange skin tone and dark hair. How could she not want this child. Carmen was so tired when the Socialworker handed her to Momma Rosa she just laid her head on her shoulder and didn't say a word. Soon she was fast asleep.

Momma Rosa had taken two weeks off from work to care for Carmen and for Carmen to get use to her. From the first time they met, it seems like they had always had a bond.

Once the two weeks were up and Momma Rosa had to return to work she put Carmen in the onsite Daycare on the second floor of her building while she reported to work on the fifth floor. Momma Rosa felt so bad that she had to leave Carmen. When she handed her over to the Daycare worker, Carmen clung to her and did not want to let go of her sweater, while screaming and crying and saying a couple of words in Spanish. She did call Momma Rosa, momma. Once the daycare worker calmed Carmen down she began playing with the other kids with toys and looking at TV. Momma Rosa would go downstairs on her lunch break and watch Carmen through the one way window observing her activities. However, when Momma Rosa picked Carmen at the end of the day, Carmen would cry and scream again, clinging to Momma Rosa. Momma Rosa began singing a song to her in Spanish and Carmen calmed down again. Each day for a week Carmen would scream, kick and cry holding on to Momma Rosa when she would drop her off at daycare. In less than two weeks, Carmen realized that Momma Rosa was not going to leave her, but she always came back. One day when Momma Rosa went to a grocery store in her neighborhood, a lady approached her and started talking and soon introduced herself and said that she was Javier's English teacher from high school. So Momma Rosa began to listen, this lady also had a background in speaking Spanish and could communicate in a way that Momma Rosa could understand. She had tutored Javier as much as she could and had invited him to her house where she had a lot of learning material, but ended up subduing him and she got pregnant, but didn't tell her husband that their son was not his, but the baby was Javier. So that was a secret that Momma Rosa did not want Carmen to know, by the time Momma Rosa found out Javier had been killed in prison. He was convicted of murder before Carmen was born and sentenced to prison for killing a Puerto Rican gang member while he was on his way home from work in the Chelsea neighborhood near 27th Street subway train station. Momma Rosa was born in a little village outside of the Capitol city in Honduras, Tegucigalpa, San Pedro Sula on September 16, 1953. Her given name was Rosa Marie Ortez. Her parents were Carlos and Lucinda Ortez, the second child of five and the oldest girl. Her education consisted of her going to a combined Elementary and Middle School and High School near by, she only completed 10th grade. She was responsible for quite a few household chores as well as helping out with the young three children. Some of Rosa's chores were sewing, cooking, feeding the children and making sure that they were properly clothed and bathe. Laundry was a task that was shared by her mother when she wasn't helping in the fields. Sometimes Rosa would go to the field with her father and brother. On days when merchandise had to be shipped, the entire family went to get the orders out. Only would the oldest two children spend most of the day working and packaging up commodities that mostly shipped to the United States. At the young age of seven Rosa could perform most of the household duties that her mother did, even cooking a complete meal. Her younger brother was only two when she began watching him and two years later a sister and finally three years later another girl. Because Honduras was such a poor country, many farmers barted for goods and services. Rosa's father exported fish as well as crops. He had hired hands that assisted him most of the times, however when they had to prepare for shipping everyone joined in to get orders out on time. Most of the things needed to ship to U.S. was supplied by the U.S. also their cargo ships were used to transport items through the U.S. Customs. Any foul play was handled at the U.S. Customs Department, it didn't always affect them, because U.S. citizens on the boats would check off on the list of items the things that met their approval. The majority of Rosa's father's income came from these type of services. The other came from locals and shipping by train and tractor trailers to Mexico and surrounding areas. Produce and livestock and fish was what supplied restaurants and grocery stores. Due to a shortage of money to run the farm, Rosa's father had a rooming house to provide lodging for the hired hands, this kept the overhead lower than if they had to pay to live some where else, they stayed for free and were given two meals a day. Few hired hands were accompanied by a family. They would have to pay a fee out of their $1 hour wages to compensate for the extra baggage. Only one family in the rooming house were allowed without any extra overhead. That was a family of at least a man to work the fields, a woman to do all the cooking and cleaning and if they had children they all would live in the one room. Only outside toilets were on property as well as outside showers. Most of the workdays consisted of ten hour shifts with two breaks and one half hour lunch. Rosa's father employed about thirty workers. Mostly locals of Honduras and a few immigrants from Central America and Mexico who came from poor regions or who lived near by. Rosa's family had few luxuries, all clothes had to be made for the ladies and children. On rare occasions her father would buy shoes for the family. Mostly boots for the boys to work on the farm. He would take them to the Capital city to get their necessary items. There was no English spoken in the home, nor the fields or the docks. The only time English was spoke was when a pick up by the U.S. boats would come or when her father and brothers would go to sell goods and services. Rosa's oldest brother would do most of the speaking when it came to communicating in English. Her father knew very little English and relied on his sons to communicate and to calculate the money. Fortunately when they received U.S. money which would be more than their current money it went a lot further. Twice a year Rosa's father allowed the children and her mother to go to Mexico to buy something special. However, her father was more about saving for "A rainy day". Most of Honduras was mountainous and lent itself to ruff terrain when it came to growing crops or having successful livestock. Fortunately they lived by the sea and the railways went through the next town, only five miles away. Rosa remembered one year when the crops were growing real good and the livestock were multiplying, a tornando with flooding water from the mountainside came down and washed a lot of the crops away and killed more than a dozen animals. Her father had to let some works go until he could recover from such devastation. Some of the farmers in our village lost everything and had to rely on the kindness of others to get by. Rosa's father eventhough he lost a great deal of his income, step in to do what he could do to help out. Besides he taught his children we in this village are all like family and we are helpers one to the other. Rosa's uncle, his fathers brother also owned a farm, not as big as Rosa's father lived in a village about three miles south of them. His name was Gustavo, he did not suffer any damage to his crops or farm animals, only minor wind and debris came across his land, he helped out quite a bit. Rosa's father had a tractor that carried a plowing and also a harvesting attachment, he also had a old farm truck for transporting the workers and gathering crates of fruit and vegetables. Rosa's father was an excellent mechanic who taught his sons to fix any type of farm equipment and personal vehicles in addition to fixing electrical problems and plumbing and carpentry. Her father believed in boys knowing everything there was to know about keeping your household in good shape. Rosa's family accepted the Catholic faith as their religion, but were not as dedicated to attending services. The nearest church was located in the Capital city, and they only attended on special occasions.

One night at Carmen's school the teachers were in charge of putting on a Fall festival together. Carmen was in charge of kicking off the festival with all the third grade children performing a play. This was on a Thursday night, on Saturday the school would be having a Carnival, called a Fall Festival to kick off the season. This annual event was to help raise money to help offset the expense of field trips. One field trip would be to take a selected group of Elementary children to Radio City Music Hall to see the Christmas Spectacular, featuring the Rockettes. This activity has been featured at Radio City Music Hall for more than 45 years. The show is very organized and spiritual. First the Piano rises out of the floor with the pianist playing holiday music accompanied by a live orchestra. The long golden pipes that are station on each side of the grand stand coming out of the ceiling is so majestic. It easy to image yourself listening to music played by angels. It's peaceful, spiritual and very dramatic. Each of the members of the orchestra is well dressed. The men all in long black Tuxedo jackets, matching pants, white button down shirts, black bow tie and well groomed. The ladies long black dresses or skirts with black tops, faces radiant and steadfast. Not one instrument is played off key or out of sort. Once the announcer comes to give the prelude and outline of the show, everything falls in place. The program goes on with the Rockettes leading the dancing. All dressed in tights, stilletos and sparkling leotards, tutus and smiles, tapping their shoes moving in a circular synchronized fashion, arms locked at the elbows and the twenty plus ladies steal the show. Their formation is perfect, it's mesmerizing. A story is brought forth by two brothers one young and another older. The older brother doesn't believe in Christmas, but the young one does and tries to convenience the older brother, that Christmas is real. A series of events take place and the older finally believes. There is a story of Bethlehem about the Christ child and his birth on Christmas and angels declaring his deatie and wisemen came to worship him as he was born in a stable. They were declaring him as the new born King. During this performance live animals are paraded on stage. Camels, donkeys, goats and even dogs cross the stage. After the biblical scene, Santa Claus appears with present and cheer, saying Ho, Ho, Ho, his signature sound, and flies away in the air. Throughout the show the Rockettes appear a number of times dancing and kicking their legs high into the air. During their grand finally, they change into red leotards, trimmed in white faux fur, with long sleeved tops red, trimmed in white faux fur, red stellitos, Christmas hat, red with white faux fur, hats leaning to one side of their head, white pom pom on the part that's hanging down. Each guess who enter the theatre are offered a Santa hat along with3-D glasses. The auditorium at Radio City Music Hall is old, each part of the hall is decorated with wall paper and drapes that have been hung for years. It is a place that you would see designed in the early 50's or 60's Early American chandelier and the bathrooms are very grand. Mirrors with vanity tables and chairs are located in the women's bathroom with setties and burgurdy carpet through the entire auditorium and antique stair rails decorated with French rod iron flowers adorn the stairway. As the evening began for the Fall Festival play, the parents were there promptly at 6:30 p.m with their children. The play was scheduled to begin at 7:00 p.m. Carmen introduced the layout of the play and began to start the scenes of the play. The children were so exited and did a good job, they received a standing ovation from the audience and were congratulated by the Head Master of the school for doing such a fine job. One of Carmen's students began walking toward her in the auditorium from the back of the room, yelling Ms. De La Cruz, while holding this gorgeous man's hand. Oh my God, it's Andy Garcia she thought. Just a little shorter than Andy but every bit as delicious looking. All dressed in his cream suit, white shirt, striped blue and brown tie, thick gold chain around his neck, gold watch, shiny shoes and a big smile. It was Mary one of her smart bright students. Once she got close to her teacher, she said this is my Uncle Venito. Carmen could smell his cologne before he reached her, it was mesmerizing. She just wanted to fall in his arms and kisses him. So Ms. De La Cruz said hi and shook his hand. He replied hi while shaking her hand. He continued with, what a great show and asked her how long did it take for her to teach the children all of the parts to the play.

Immediately she gave recognizition to all the participants and that it was not just her doing. As they were continuing to talk, another student came up with his parents and wanted them to meet his teacher, it was Tommy Thomas, another bright student. So not to be rude, Venito said that maybe we could talk another time and Carmen said that would be good and said good bye to him. The week-end had passed, Carmen thought for sure she would see him at the school Carnival, but only Mary and her mother showed up, with her baby brother. The baby was crying and Mary's mom seemed to be aggravated by his behavior, so Mary only waved and before Carmen knew it they were gone. Carmen spent the entire week-end thinking about Venito. She just could not get him out of her head. Monday morning when Carmen arrived at school, before clocking in, she notice a small vase with a half dozen roses and babies breast and greenery. She commented to the receptionist about how lovely her flowers were and how lucky she was to receive them so early in the week. The receptionist, Lizzie just chuckled and said, they are for you.

Carmen's eyes lite up like a firecracker, then she leaned in an smelled their sweet aroma, she thought I could just get lost in their fragrance, she said hum. Who would be giving me flowers, in her mind she thought, I received them from the principal for the play on Thurday night. She proceeded to read the card. And the card said, It was nice meeting you on Thursday night. If you are not seeing anyone please give me a call. Remember I'm Mary's Uncle. Signed: V along with a cell phone number. It took Carmen two weeks before she tried to contact Venito. The conversation started off, "Carmen speaking", I missed placed your number and was afraid once I found it again that you wouldn't remember me." "Venito speaks", I thought that you had a boyfriend and went on about your business. I am glad that you called, because I want to invite you to coffee. Carmen speaks, I would love to go for coffee some evening after work and on a day when I didn't have a class. Venito, so what are you studying, Carmen, well I'm getting my Master's and will be finished by Spring. Venito, just let me know what is the best time for you.

Carmen speaks, any day but Wednesday. Most of my work is done online, but Wednesday, I have to report to New York State University to do some site work. Venito speaks, how about next

Thursday, after you leave work. Are you familiar with Carnegie Deli at 56th Street and 7th Avenue. Carmen speaks, of course I can meet you there at 6:30 p.m. So it's a go says Venito. Yes says Carmen. So after their phone conversation Venito began to dance around with overwhelming excitement and say out loud, "I have a date with the most beautiful girl in the world named, Carmen. To Venito, Carmen reminded him of Michelle Rodriquez who played in Fast and Furious, she was gorgeous. Also Carmen was overcome with joy and began counting the days and hours until she meet up with Venito, she thought to herself, he is the most handsome man that I have ever met and he want to have coffee with me. She felt so special, it was as if she was the Queen of England. The day of their date, Carmen made sure the night before that she packed everything in a catch all bag to change her clothes at school before her date. From her head to her toe, she wanted to make a good impression with Venito and wanted him to have a memory of her beauty burned in his head. That morning before leaving the house, she made sure that Momma Rosa knew that she would be going on a date and would not be coming home as early as she normally do on Thursday. Again she reminded Momma Rosa so that she would not worry. Besides, Momma Rosa gave her freedom to go and come as a young adult and never wanted to stand in her way if it meant her having a chance for happiness. Momma Rosa was proud of Carmen's accomplishments and trusted her to make good choice about friends especially men. After Carmen had made the date with Venito on the phone, she decided to tell Momma Rosa about him and what she knew of him. It was not like Momma Rosa to interfere with any conversation Carmen had on the phone, unless she felt Carmen was disturbed by it and sometimes, even then she tried to mine her own business. Because of their close relationship, Carmen would tell her anyway what was on her mind. Growing up Momma Rosa said to Carmen, "I don't care what it is you are facing, GOOD or BAD, we can get through it if we stick together." Venito and Carmen continued to see each other on a weekly basis for about two months, then more often after that, three or more times a week. Before they knew it it was Christmas. Venito had always been a gentlemen and feels that he wanted to let Carmen know how special she was. So he asked her how would she like to go away with him for the holidays once school was out. Without hesitation, she reply with a loud YES. Venito said, you don't know where we are going nor do you know how long we will be gone. Carmen replied, "I don't care, along as it's away from here." Carment had never been overnight anywhere except when her and some of her teacher friends went to Maryland for a bachelorette party and a wedding, where she was one of the bridesmaids. So going anywhere with Venito, who she was falling in love with was an added benefit. To keep the suspence going, Venito said, I'll tell you tomorrow and you can let me know if the time frame work for you. Carmen tossed and turned all night, waiting to meet up with Venito to tell her where they were going. It was Saturday and they were meeting for breakfast and then going to a preseason game at Madison Square Garden. The Jets were playing the Raiders. She had planned to spend the whole day with him. At last Venito made it to where Carmen lived and picked her up several times before meeting Momma Rosa. Venito hired a limo and pulled up to her apartment, got out and went up to her third floor apartment. He knocked on the door and waited for someone to come. Because Carmen was expecting him and Momma Rosa waited patiently in the livingroom for him to come in after Carmen opened the door. Venito was a bit nervous to meet her grandmother and was afraid she would ask him all sorts of questions. He knew how important it was for her to know who Carmen was seeing and to know if he was a nice guy. Once Carmen opened the door, Venito said, WOW, Carmen's long brunette/reddish hair was curled with big falling locks, make-up impeccable with red lips and long eye lashes, bright white teeth. She had on a Channel off white blouse with bell sleeves, a three tier silver necklace draped with diamond, one with a single diamond and one herrinbone chain. Her earrings were silver, one a half inches long, three quarter moon shape with diamonds. A tennis bracelet was visiable on her left hand along with a single diamond ring a promise ring from Venito. She wore a black leather mini skirt, rhinestones on each side of the skirt, black sheer stockings and black stilettos rhinestone buckles. Venito was dressed in A Versage off white pullover sweater long sleeves with Versage logo in upper left near top, dress black jeans by Versage as well as Armani loafers, black. Gold chain and a Rolex watch and Cartier gold ring. He was cleanly shaven hair trimmed on side top of head locks draping toward the front of his head. His cologne was Preston Watson he looked and smelled so good. She greeted Venito with a big smile and said, how are you, then she reached out to him with both arms extended and grabbed him with his arms down by his side and pecked him on the lips with her lips. Not even a minute had passed when she brought him around to the livingroom where Momma Rosa was sitting and introduced him. He was so nervous after finally seeing her, that he called her Momma Rosa. So Momma Rosa was a little shocked by him addressing her that way after Carmen had told him her full name. She gave him a smirk but quickly changed it into a smile. She was very impressed by how nice he was and the fact that he brought her a gift. Momma Rosa did not say too much to him because her English was not that good. However, she did use Carmen to translate some of her conversation.

Momma Rosa always had some type of baked good in the house and told Carmen to invite him for some breakfast tea cookies and coffee. However, he declined and said that he would take her up on that another time. She spoke in English and said that he was welcome in her home anytime. Those words meant a lot to Venito as well as Carmen. So Venito said that we had a busy day and needed to get going. Before walking out of the door, he spoke in Spanish and told Momma Rosa that it was nice meeting her. Out of the squeaky door they went, walking down the wooden stairway to the street. Right in front of Carmen's apartment building was a stretched black limo waiting, door helded open by the driver and soft music playing, "You are so beautiful to me", by Blake Shelton.

Carmen looked at Venito and got teary eyed and said did you do this just for me. Venito smiling back and said yes, just for you. Again Carmen hugged him and they proceeded to get in the limo. Because Venito always like surprising her, she was anxious and wanted to ask where they were going for breakfast, but she did not want to interfer with his surprise. Once inside the limo, Carmen noticed a bouquet of flowers, her favorite yellow roses, again her eyes filled up with tears. Venito just kissed her face softly. As the car went down 9th Avenue turning on 34th Street toward downtown New York City, Carmen observed people walking going into Macy's and the many surrounding stores. Saturday is always filled with excitment in New York, there were side showing where people would gather to be mesmerized by a magician and a informercials selling gimmicks pitch by an new businesses, even dance offs. The biggest excitement would be in the evening in Times Square. People from various parts of the country, international tourist and locals to interact and watch multiple events taking place. Music would be playing, people dancing, eating from the street vendors, going in and out of deparment stores restuaranats such as Star Bucks, Ray's Pizza, Applebees, and more. Times Square can be very exciting and fun most of the time, it can also be dangerous there is always thieves preying on unsuspecting tourist and locals who are not paying attention to their values. You must be paying attention. One good thing, there are cameras everywhere, along with police, security and other law enforcement personnel to be on guard for violent activity. As I recognized all of the buildings that we were passing, I knew we were headed downtown somewhere. And to my surprise, we stopped in front of the Empire State Building. As a kid I had visited there once and did not think about going there as an adult. I didn't know that it had a breakfast restaurant in it. After 911, it became the largest building in New York City, since the World Trade Center. The limo driver rushed over to open the back door and Carmen stepped out first. Venito was within inches of stepping out behind her. He said to Carmen we are here. As they entered the building Carmen always pay attention to the deco of a building and try to interpret what the artist was thinking with certain artwork that is on display. She observed when she walked through the door, a sculture that was done by Astric Boesman of a mosaic butterfly, seven feet tall, outlined in gold glass, each section of the butterfly had different colors and glistered as the light above it circled around it. Another piece of artwork was an apple about five feet tall, with red color and brown line zig zag through the entire apple. Also she tried to interpret what the artist was saying. Some of the pieces were done by students from Metropolitan University of Arts and Design. Carmen did not want to tarry any longer as to not spoil Venito's surprise. A building like the Empire State Building was one of the many buidings that was under heavy security and you had to have clearance and a reservation to even be allowed in the building as well as proper identification and be scanned as well as your picture taken by cameras. Once you were cleared, you were escorted to your destination by another roving security personnel. As they got on the elevator with the security officer, they went up to the roof top restaurant. The name of the restaurant was Chantillies. As they entered the restaurant, the security officer backed into the elevator and a restaurant host greeted them by name. It was brunch time at Chantillies. As they entered the seating area, Carmen looked ahead and saw that there was a panoramic view of New York City. It looked so peaceful. She looked down at the harbor she saw people loading and unloading boats, looking out at the water on the East River, there was a ship headed for shore as well as the Staten Island ferries. One going to Staten Island, while one passed the other headed back to New York harbor. Also at a distance were sailboats and fishing boats doing what they do on a nice cool Saturday morning, some were fishing while others were just enjoying the scenery. The decorations in the restaurant were paintings that were done by artist, some from the same school as the art downstairs in the lobby. Each table had a small bouquet of flowers, roses and babies breath along with fern to complete each arrangement. There was classical music playing in the overhead speakers, people chatting and laughing as the waiters and waitresses took their order. In addition, there was a small emsumbro of musicians coming around to each table playing a mandolin, harp and accordion taking request. The atmosphere was perfect. Once the order of beverage was taken of Momosa, Champagne, Coffee and Tea, Venito and Carmen had small talk about the weeks activities. Again Carmen thanked him for a nice morning outing. Venito said a person such as yourself deserved the best that life had to offer. Her containment could not be held back any longer. She looked at Venito with eyes stretched wide and insisted that he say where they were going for the holidays. It was the end of October and she needed to buy somethings for the trip. Without further adure, Venito answered her by saying, we are going to Las Vegas for nine days. Carmen let out a short scream and said in reply, Las Vegas., Wow I didn't image going there. Venito said that he had to go for a conference and wanted her to be his special guest. He wanted to show her off to his business partners and she looked good next to him and he knew that they would be jealous to see him with such a pretty girl. This is a vacation that many only dream of, Carmen began to think, I wonder if he is going to propose and then marry her in Las Vegas. The game at Madison Square Gardens did not show a favorable win for New York and the couple left early disappointed and went for a stroll at Brooklyn Botanical Gardens to pass the time away before Carmen returned home to be with Momma Rosa. She was very dedicated to taking care of her grandmother and didn't want her to want for anything. Brooklyn Botanical Gardens was so peaceful and colorful this time of year. They knew that the flowers would soon fade away and winter with its snow would blanket over them. The first time Carmen went to the Garden was when she accompanied a class on a field trip there. The portion that most intrigued her was the children's garden area, where they were able to plant a vegetable in a pot and then bring back to the school to take care and then take home to continue to let it grow and be able to harvest whatever it yielded. Of course once some of the children took their plants home, they died while others were very responsible and was able to report that they were able to harvest something off of their plant. Carmen finally finished her Master's Degree program and was relived that she had gotten a higher degree, which meant more money.

Weeks had passed by and Venito was staying out later and later. His reasons for that is that his father was getting sicker and sicker and he had to attend to some of his father's affairs. So Carmen went along with it and notice that Venito was not bringing her as many presents since they moved in together. Venito said that he was under a lot of pressure and it slip his mind and for her to get off his back. Carmen had notice a big change in his personality since they moved in several months ago. He stop picking up his dirty clothes, he was having a drink everyday that he come home and be bitchy about every little thing. How could this wonderful person all of a sudden change and treat her bad. He made no excuses as to why he acted the way he did. Instead he wanted Carmen to think that she was doing some wrong. One night Carmen had fixed a special dinner for Venito, some of his favorite desserts, such as Tirusumi, whoopee pies, and egg custard pie. She bought them from the deli near their apartment, called Palermo's. Palmero's sold some of the most gorgeous desserts in all of New York City and the Bronx. They were located a block on the other side of the street from their apartment. Off and on for awhile, Carmen and Venito was having a heated discuss and he did not want to address the issue that she inquired about. She wanted to know what took him so long to get home after telling her that he would be their by 6:00p.m. She had prepared a nice dinner of Beef Wellington, with new potatoes, fresh green beans and sweet rolls. This English dish of strip steak wrapped in puff pasty was one of his all time favorite dishes. One of his favorite vegetables was fresh green beans and potatoes. Carmen had taken a cooking class to learn how to prepare some of his favorite dished and was not happy that he did acknowledge the trouble she went through to prepare it. She left work early just to get all of the ingredients for it and that damn class cost her $350.00 for a two day four hour course. She was so mad that she wrapped everthing in foil and threw it in the trash. How do like that,

I spent a whopping $109.85 on the meal and desserts just to have you come home when you felt like it, that is so disrespectful she yelled. Venito yelling back and said you don't understand what I have to go through to make you happy and all you do is complain. Shortly, Venito received a phone call on his cell phone. When he saw the name and number he knew it was going to be another argument with another female. He went into the livingroom from the diningroom of their apartment. He started talking low and slow, then his voice elevated, by this time Carmen had gone into their bedroom and closed the door. Venito greeted the caller with, How did you get this number. The caller on the other end was crying and yelling at him, but it did not slow him down asking her questions about how she got the number. On his end all he knew was that he had gave her money to take care of something and she didn't do it. He promised her that if she didn't take care of it, he would take care of her. Venito told Carmen that he was going out and didn't know when he would be back and for her not to put the apartment alarm on.

Carmen did not answer him as he left, but threw herself on her bed and began to cry. It was about 1230 a.m. when Venito returned. By this time Carmen had gone to sleep.

Around 4:30 a.m. Venito was fast asleep, snoring and grunting. Carmen took this opportunity to go to the bathroom and to check his phone to find out who he was talking to earlier. She knew very little of his friends and business partners. But knew that he periodically called his aunt and his sister. The female name that she saw on his phone, she did not recognize. So she took a picture of his list of resent calls and went back to bed. The next morning around 5:30 a.m. Venito got up at his usual time to get dressed for work. Carmen was still sleeping or so he thought. By 6:00 a.m. Venito was leaving the house. Carmen got up at 6:00 a.m. She sat on the side of the bed and stretched her arms over her head and sighed. She was thinking, who is Maria Vega. I don't think that his clerk in his Manhattan store, nor was it the clerk in his Brooklyn or Soho store. His Harlem store was run by blacks and that doesn't sound like a black persons name.

Carmen had decided that she would place a call to this Maria Vega when she left school today. It was about 4:15 that evening that Carmen placed a call to Maria Vega to find out who she was. After several rings, Maria Vega answered. Carmen said who she was and didn't know if her and Venito were friends. Maria quickly said, I know who you are in an angry voice. She said that you are that bitch that Venito is talking about marrying. But he is expecting a child with me, so don't get your hopes up honey. I got this man by the balls. Immediately, chills ran up and down Carmen's spine and she became very angry with Maria, and slammed her phone closed. Carmen in a fit of rage, balled up her fist with bent arms keeping them firm began to rant and fume saying who do she think she is, Venito belong to me. Once Carmen left work she took the M7 bus to Central Park. Before she met Venito, she would go to Central Park in the evenings to walk through some of the flower and water gardens. It was a peaceful place to be when you needed to cool off. Eventhough it was filled with people, no one harassed you. Yes there was always homeless people there, begging for spare change. Carmen was use to saying no and moved on to complete her walk. She made sure to be done with her walk before night fall. Central Park is a very dangerous place to be after dark. Just the week before her walk, a man and a woman got stabbed by a thief, trying to take her purse. Luckly, they suffered minor injuries and manage to hold on to her purse. A New York City policeman was near by and gave chase to the suspect. The suspect got away, but the couple gave a detail description of the man and a day later, he was shot by police and died on the scene. It was said that he was a crack head and was seeking money to buy more drugs. When Carmen got home, Venito was waiting for her which was unusual, he never comes home before her. He was eating dinner that he had picked up from one of the local take out restaurants. As Carmen came through the door Venito was sitting with his mouth filled with food. Carmen said hello. Venito gave her a look, as they say, "IF LOOKS COULD KILL", was his expression through his eyes. She wanted to know why he was home early. Once Venito emptied his mouth, he called her over from looking at today's mail and told her to sit down, so she did, right next to him. He asked her, who did you call today. She looked him dead in the eyes and said, no one. Venito said a woman called my Soho store and said that you called her and threatened her. I need to know the truth, Venito said. Are you sure you didn't talk to a lady named Maria Vega, Carmen got tripped up and said I had the wrong number. Why would I call her I don't even know her. Venito looked at Carmen pointing his finger toward Carmen in anger saying stay the HELL out of my business. It was right then that Carmen knew that she was dealing with a dangerous man and he could really hurt her. That night Venito left the apartment after talking to Carmen, but did not tell her that he was coming back. Carmen tossed and turned all night not sure if she would be there alone all night. The back up alarm went off at 5:30 as always on a weekday morning, but there was no Venito. She looked around, and his side of the bed had not been disturbed. As she always do, she woke up to her back up alarm at 6:00 a.m. and got dressed for her teaching job at her school. Dragging herself from their second floor apartment to the sidewalk outside of their building, to the subway entry two blocks away, back up to the street level and on to the school campus where she worked, Carmen thought I have never been so tired in all my days as a teacher. The receptionist greeted her with a GOOD MORNING!, and Carmen just looked away. The receptionist called her name, saying "Carmen are you alright", Carmen apologized and said she didn't get that much rest last night and needed a pick me up) She had about 30 minutes before her student came into the classroom and did not want to look sad. So the receptionist got Carmen a cup of coffee and a warm towel. Carmen said thank you to the receptionist and continued drinking the coffee. Most mornings Carmen would have a cup of green tea and a bagel. But this particular morning she needed coffee. The receptionist told Carmen if she needed to talk on her break while the children were at specials, she would be glad to listen. Carmen agreed and said that she would return during that time.

She knew that she could count on the receptionist to be a good listening ear. For several weeks now Venito had been asking strange towards Carmen not talking to her, leaving dirty dishes in the sink, staying out all times of night and some times not coming home at all. When Carmen asked him what was wrong he would speak angrily and said nothing, that he just had to take care of his father and because he is gone so late, he would just stay at his sister's to not wake her up at night. Carmen also asked him did he want her to leave and he said no. So she decided to try being as nice as she could to him. Although, she missed him at night. He was the reason that she would get a good night's rest.

Because he would be sleeping next to her and caressing her and massaging her body all over.

As Carmen was walking to the subway on a Friday morning on her way to school, a woman began walking and talking to her. The conversation was quite pleasant and then the woman, said don't look directly at her but let's pretend that the conversation is still good and listen to me as I tell you a story. The woman was Debbie from the FBI. As she began to tell Carmen that Venito is part of an organized crime family, Carmen nodded her head forward as if to say yes. Debbie went on to say, that they had been watching his activities for months and how he interacted with several organized crime families and how they were responsible for a number of murders and drug trafficking, human sex trafficking, arson, racketeer stolen merchandise from cargo ships airplanes landing with merchandise from forgeign countries and many more serious crime activities. The FBI have had Venito and Carmen under surveillance ever since they moved in together. The families have been doing business in the state as well as other U.S. states, Canada, Mexico, Europe and Spain. The FBI had evidence, but not enough to convict anyone.

However, Debbie said that they didn't know how much Carmen was involved, but needed to isolate her from the equation. Debbie showed her an FBI badge that she had hidden inside a binder and told Carmen that she would be in contact with her again. Once they got to the subway, Debbie got on a separate train from Carmen. Carmen was in shock and disbelief of all that the agent told her, she was nervous about seeing Venito again. Her thoughts were, to figure out how to get away from him without him suspecting that she maybe talking to the FBI. All day long at school all she could think about her relationship with Venito, sometimes she loved him, some times she hated him. Carmen finished the day at school and rushed home to pack a weekend bag. She left Venito a note and told him that Momma Rosa was not feeling good and that she was spending the weekend with her, to take care of her. Sure enough Carmen was not lying, Momma Rosa had been to the doctor the day before and was told to take it easy for a day or two. She was diagnosed with fatigue and low blood. When Momma Rosa spoke on the phone to Carmen and was told she was coming for the weekend, she was thrilled. Carmen asked her what did she want for dinner and Momma Rosa, said she was not hungry and also that she had something around the house to eat if she got hungry. Carmen knew that Momma Rosa liked Italian food and she liked soup. So Carmen decided to stop at a deli near Momma Rosa's building that served a variety of food items. The name of the deli was Zora's Delicatessan. Before Carmen could reach the deli about a block away, the aroma of sausage and peppers being cooked on a grill captured her nostrils and her stomach decided it was party time and aroused her taste buds. Carmen entered the doors of the deli as two Jewish gentlemen were coming out and greeted her with a hello in English, while their conversation was being spoken to each other in a German dialect. The atmosphere in the deli was noisy as customers were in line trying to decide what they were going to order, the cashiers were shouting orders to the cooks, the wait and waitresses were picking up and serving the seated customers and German polka music was being played coming out of the speakers on the ceiling. Some of the seated customers were speaking and laughing in different languages, Spanish, German, Yiddish, Italian, French and other language Carmen wasn't familiar with. She had studied different languages and had a minor in Foreign Language and a

Major in Elementary Education. Her Master's Degree allowed her the freedom to work on a University level, but she loved Elementary school best. Once Carment reached the show case with all the items on display that was being serviced that day, she could not make up her mind what she would have. There were all kinds of salads, there were garden salad, macaroni salad, tuna salad, antipasta salad, German potato salad, and many more. As she looked down the show case, next to the salads, there was a hot food section with yellow rice, white rice, macaroni and cheese, vegetable medley of broccoli, cauliflower and carrots, green beans, white beans, stew beef with carrots and potatoes in gravy, mash potatoes, corn, cabbage, fried fish, baked chicken, sausage and peppers, pasta with sauce, carrots and chicken pot pies. The desserts were always the first thing you saw in the display case as well as on top of the display case when you entered the deli. Each week they would feature a different dessert at a reduced price. This week the featured dessert was bread pudding with rum raisin sauce, Momma Rosa's favorite. There were only a few desserts on display and Carmen new that the deli would run out of desserts before the night was over, and you would have to wait until Sunday to get fresh home made desserts. They never ran out of ice-cream, that would be what you had if you wanted dessert when they ran out. Usually on Friday, Momma Rosa and her had some type of fish to honor the Catholic tradition, however once she and Venito got together, she was accustomed to fine dining on the week-end.

But she didn't want to forget where she came from so she ditched the idea of sausage and peppers. She decided on a meal plate of grilled white fish, seasoned rice, cabbage and carrots. She rarely ate bread and decided to take the bread that came along with her meal to give it to Momma Rosa. The deli always served some type of soup, so she decided on the Seafood soup for Momma Rosa, she ordered her a large soup, so that Momma Rosa could save for another time. Besides, she knew her grandmother well enough to know that the large would be too much for one meal. In less than ten minutes of placing her order, Carmen was on her way to Momma Rosa's apartment. The streets were lined with vendors selling some knock off merchandise of purses, jewelry, clothes, fake designer sunglasses, CDs and other items. Some of the vendors were legite sales people and there were others who didn't have a license. Very rare the police bothered with them unless there was a complaint of violence and weapons being displayed. Some of the vendors were from weekend cargo ships some of the crew would get off the docked boats with there merchandise, mostly CD and fake designer merchandise to make some New York money. Tourist who visited New York everyday were always looking for a bargain, and would walk the street at night looking for souvenirs. They would spend outrageous amount of money, because the vendor told them it was real. As we New Yorkers know, most of the merchandise was import from China and sold in bulk. China was given a right of passage to bring their ships into harbor and sell their merchandise wholesale at a much more affordable price than what America could make it for. As Carmen passed through a parade of shoppers she reached Momma Rosa's building and opened to exterior door into a square 4x by 4x foyer. Up the stairs she went until she reached the third floor. As she was walking up the stairs she could hear people in different apartments, there was a baby crying, children laughing and shouting having a good time playing video games, a woman and man, arguing about money, music being played so loud that you couldn't hear yourself think, and a ball being bounced against a wall. Two ladies at different times came down stairs as Carmen was going up, one of the ladies recognized Carmen and had a brief conversation with her and asked had she gotten married yet and she said not yet and said that she has been promised, showing the ring, the other lady said, hi but was rushing down the stairs after her two children. They were going to the movies.

Eventhough Carmen had a key, she knocked on the door. Momma Rosa said, Carmen is that you, she reply as she opened the door, yes and Carmen said Ola Momma Rosa, how are you. Momma Rosa said she was fine, but needed to get some rest, Carmen said I brought you some soup and bread pudding. Momma Rosa was so excited. Momma Rosa rarely ate take out food. She tried to buy all that she needed each week at the grocery store. They hugged and Carmen kissed Momma Rosa on the cheek after she put their food on the dining room table. Both of them were so excited to be spending the week-end together that conversation at that time was more important than eating. Carmen was curious to know what Momma Rosa was doing to make herself sick. Momma Rosa kind of brushed it off as to say she didn't want to talk about it. Of course she was more interested in what was going on with Carmen and Venito. Carmen did not want to tell Momma Rosa that Venito is involved in some heavy shit and that she was contacted by the FBI. It was important to Carmen that she kept things from Momma Rosa as much as possible, she knew she would worry. Momma Rosa was a little reluctant to tell Carmen what she thought about Venito and how she knew about his family. Carmen was so happy when she introduced him to her and wanted Momma Rosa to like him. Momma Rosa had taught Carmen well and knew that down the road that she would find out things about him, but hope that her heart would not be broken once she found out. She loved her very much and would always be there for her no matter what. It was midnight on a Sunday night and Venito was coming into the apartment and Carmen was up going over some school paperwork. He brought her a bouquet of flowers and said hello to her, then said I thought you would be in the bed by now. He kissed her on the cheek and sat down on the sofa next to her and ask her what she was doing. She said she was studying a standardized testing booklet that the children had to do next month and she would be one of the proctors for the fourth grade. Her part would be to administer the language arts portion of the test as well as tutor some of the kids. Venito was not interested in that and began kissing her on her next and she accommodated him, she knew that he was ready for sex and did not want to do too much talking. It had been a while since they were intimate and she did not want to think about any thing else, but making love to him.

They both went to the bedroom and pleasured each other. The chit chat continued from the livingroom only Venito wanted to apologize for his behavior and let her know that he really loved her and wanted to spend the rest of his life with her. Carmen responded and said that she wanted to spend the rest of her life with him and wanted to know what could she do to make him happy. The answer is simply he said, just stay beautiful. Two weeks had passed and the arguing and disagreement between Carmen and Venito picked back up, but this time he was coming home drunk and finally lashed out at her with a slap across the face. He immediately apologized and said he never wanted to hurt her, and he went to bed. Agent Debbie got a job at Carmen's school as a substitute teacher, and saw Carmen on a regular basis. They had lunch together after the second day of Agent Debbie's assignment there. At this time, Agent Debbie showed Carmen some pictures of Venito and a woman named Maria Vega. She asked Carmen if she knew this woman, and Carmen said no she didn't know the woman, but took a picture of Venito's contacts in his phone and her name and number was one that I dialed the next day after Venito was arguing with her. What I heard him say to her was, either you get rid of it or I'll get rid of you. Agent Debbie said, she's dead. Carmen in a low voice said, O no, why, how. Agent Debbie said Venito had something to do with it, but he did not directly do the crime. She was telling her friends that she was pregnant from him and that she was having his first child. She was a known drug addicted and was found by her sister a couple of days ago with a needle in her arm, an overdose of herion. She was living in an apartment that was being paid for by Venito's family. She had a fake job with them as one of the receptionist at one of his office supply stores, then she filed for disability, because she had lupus and couldn't work any long. The coverage that she had was from a shady insurance company that covered her disability, also owned by one of the mob families. Agent Debbie said to Carmen, your life is in danger. Venito along with some of the other family members are trying to tie up some loose ends and you may get caught in the cross fire. Again Carmen in disbelief, did not know what she was going to do. She believe Agent Debbie but she also loved Venito inspite of his angry behavior and him lashing out at her by slapping her. Carmen asked herself, could he be at the point of really harming me. She thought about Momma Rosa, could he harm her. I don't want to put her in that type of danger.

Carmen told Agent Debbie she have got to protect her grandmother. Agent Debbie, said that they would put an agent on it and in the meantime she need to act normal and stay calm, until they let her know what she need to do to stay safe. Venito was very careful not to expose Carmen to his criminal actions and tried to act normal, however, she could tell that he was nervous about something. Could he be involved in all that Agent Debbie said, did he actually have Maria Vega killed. Carmen was more confused than ever about her future with Venito and knew that she had to be really vigiliant of his behavior as to not upset him. As Agent Debbie said, just act normal and keep your cool. Carmen greeted Venito when he arrived home that evening with a kiss and a are you hungry. As usual he either said yes or no and sat on the sofa eating junk. Normally she would fuss about him saying he was not hungry and then proceeded to eat junk. But instead, she just sat beside him and said I know that you are under a lot of pressure, do you want to talk about it. He opened up to her just a little bit, but gave her deceiving information. He told her that his business was going bankrupt and he didn't know what to do to prevent it. He would have to close at least one of his four store in order to stay afloat. Also he said that families of his employees are depending on the income generated by the sales of the office supply stores. So Carmen suggested, maybe you could alternate their schedule to give them days off without it effecting their income. As Venito thought, maybe that is a good idea. Carmen pulled her legs up on the couch and leaned on Venito's shoulder as if she was trying to be intimate. He took his arm that was leaning in her direction and cuddled her and stroked her long burnette hair. He got quiet after saying, let not talk about my troubles but I want to hear about how you are doing. Carmen said that she was excited about helping the kids prepare for the standardized test that were coming up in a couple of weeks. She was in the process of making up practice test that would prepare the children for the real test. She said that the booklet that the proctors were given can be a little confusing when it came to explaining to the children the questions and how they should answer. Most of the tests were multiple choice, but there is a written portion that must be rewritten, correcting the errors in the paragraphs. She was not the only proctor that had a problem with the sample booklets. The only things that the proctors are allowed to do once the testing starts is to read the information for a child that had problems with the wording. However, the proctors can not give any examples to the children that lead to the proctor replacing the words with a solution. Anyway, after Carmen had finish talking about the testing, Venito was falling asleep, and she said did you hear what I was talking about. And he said yes, and kissed her on the forehead. Yes he loved her very much, no he was not about to discuss his involvement with the murder of Maria Vega.

Things had heated up pretty good between Carmen and Venito. By the time he realized that Carmen had found out about Maria Vega's murder and some other organized crime activities and that the FBI were looking for evidence to convict members of his family as well as members of other mobs. The latest body was found down off River Side Drive, in Harlem upper west side near the Viaduct, located near the Hudson River. The body was identified as Ocasio Bennet, known to have ties with the Irish mob of Brooklyn. No direct witnesses to the crime, but he was located in a heavy drug infested neighborhood and some young black males and latino's were spotted running from that area. Cameras were not directly located in that area, but footage show several young men leaving the area. Ocasio Bennet had no identification on him, but his body was matched by his fingerprints that were in the NYPD file, as well as his dental records. It is believed, that the young men leaving the area may have robbed him, but there is no for sure evidence, if they actually killed him. The police are searching for the young men now. The two guys were wearing hoodies and the third and fourth guy had gang signs tattooed in their hair.

Also, the police cruiser that patrol the area at 11:00 p.m. in that area noticed an oversize black trash bag quite large in size along River Side Drive, but thought nothing of it, since the city sanitation workers, periodically collected trash and bag it up to be picked up later by sanitation trucks. Bennett's body was mangled and tied up in a large black trash bag. Carmen had moved back in with Momma Rosa claiming she was sick and needed her help. Which was true, but Momma Rosa was not about to tell Carmen what was really going on with her, because she knew Carmen would not agree to go into the Witness Protection Program, to save her own life. Venito had finally threatened to kill Carmen after she saw the news on television about poor Maria Vega dying of an overdose. Venito knew Carmen was pretty smart and would be suspicious of what could have happened.

The news had described the death as foul play. Venito was inquirying about Carmen's wearabouts at all times, he finally had her followed when she was leaving the house in the morning and when she left school in the afternoon. And he appeared to be home more than usual to see if she was talking to some one. Apparently he was aware that the FBI was trying to find out information from anyone who was close to any mob families. It had been over two years that they were tracking mob activities and trying to get enough evidence from different ones. It was believe that Ocasio was in the middle of making a deal with the FBI for protection for him and his family. Also, last year a Federal Agent was killed in a violent car crash on the George Washington Parkway bridge upper level, between him and a semi tractor trailer. The driver of the truck was never found, he fled the scene. Jerry Montana was headed home from work to Stamford Connecticut for the week-end. He never made it and the bureau was devastated. He was the closest person to crack the case against the Zambie Family, a prominent mob family who operated mostly in lower Manhattan, near Chinatown. All the evidence that he had collected was never found. His home in Connecticut had been ramsacked, while his wife was in Florida visiting her mother and his son and daughter were away at college in Princeton and Yale. The case was put on hold, no one wanted to pick up where he left off. Once Carmen had totally left Venito and moved back with Momma Rosa, she feared for her life and Agent Debbie assured her that she was only a phone call away and that she was being watched by the FBI and by Venito's people. Venito tried calling Carmen several times to come back home, however, she said that Momma Rosa was very sick. Which she was and needed to see a doctor each week for test. Momma Rosa finally told Carmen, that she had breast cancer, but it was not that bad and that chemotherapy once a week and radiation that would follow for a total of six weeks would get rid of the cancer, without any surgery. Carmen began to cry when Momma Rosa told her this and apologized that she was not there for her. Momma Rosa was not one for feeling sorry for herself nor did she teach Carmen to feel sorry for herself nor her. Carmen thought she would take care of Momma Rosa by going to her appointments and make sure she ate the right kind of food. Because Momma Rosa was a senior citizen at this time, there were a number of services that provided transportation to her chemotherapy and doctor appointments. Momma Rosa did not want Carmen to take out time from work to look after her. Sure enough a Home Healthcare Nurse was assigned to her on a twelve hour basis. Darla Romeo was the first nurse that came and would be with her from 7:00 a.m. to 7:00 p.m. Monday through Friday. Another nurse Linda Williams alternated days with Nurse Darla. Carmen decided that she did not want anyone looking after her at night. The scheduled worked out well for Carmen because she was able to get to work and back home in between the times that the nurses were there. Venito came by Momma Rosa apartment on Saturday to see how she was doing and to give her flowers and bread pudding from Zora's, also he wanted to see Carmen and to figure out if she had been appoarched by the FBI, and if so, what did she tell them. Carmen answered the door and was very polite and said hello. She did not let him in, she told him that Momma Rosa was not up for receiving company. Venito looked at Carmen with puppy dog eyes, drooped in sadness and told her that he loved her and he hoped Momma Rosa feels better. Carmen said thank you and that she would give Momma Rosa the message. There was a take down of mafia families, that ended in a shoot out, between the FBI, NYPD, special agents and SWAT. Venito was not involved, but was told that he was in hiding and seeking to eliminate her because she had been close to him and thought that she had ratted him and his family out. Venito's father was taken into custody eventhough he was on an oxygen machine and had a half lung. His Uncle Peter was being held on unrelated charges, his sister's husband, who had been Venito's business partner in his Brooklyn Office Supply Store was brought in for questioning and several other store managers, including Leroy who was over his Harlem store. There was little evidence of the store managers that the FBI was able to hold them on, other than the financial books being a little off. Each manager of the four stores, had to sit with an accountant and an auditor to go over some suspicious account activity. The family was very careful to keep the business of the stores, separate from the criminal trail of lies, murders, money laundrying, offshore seizures of international merchandise and many more crimes. Agent Debbie approached Carmen at work and said that we need to get you out of New York no later than tomorrow night. She said Venito has put out a hit on you and he is more than capable of following through on this debt. You have become a direct link to his cover. A cover that would show you being apart of his murdering and lying. Debbie told Carmen to say good-bye to Momma Rosa, because she would not see her again. She need to severe ties to anything and anyone who knew of her identity. Carmen had already prepared Momma Rosa for what was about to happen and Momma Rosa had told Carmen she need to do what the FBI said and that she would be alright. The night had come and Agent Debbie met Carmen after work, she was leaving work in a disguise to go to John F. Kennedy Airport. She would not be allowed in the airport until her flight left. Her flight was on a private FBI jet, that would take her to her destination. Agent Debbie would be her only contact to get her set up in the Witness Protection Program and would stay with her until she got to the desinated airport. It would be there Carmen and Agent Debbie would not see each other again. Carmen was not allowed to bring anything that tied her to New York or Momma Rosa. As they boarded the jet, there were only ten people on the plane, four of them were Federal Agents, the others, two pilots, and four in the Witness Protection Program. A man his wife and their five year old son, were being entered into the program. However, Agent Debbie was not in charge of that family. Also, they were not going to the same place as Carmen. There were no introductions and Carmen's only conversation and communication was with Agent Debbie. The flight took four and half hours to complete. The family got off of the plane first and the little boy was asleep in his father's arms. Yes they looked scared and weary just like Carmen. Once Carmen's bag was retrieved from the plane, Agent Debbie took her to a waiting van on the tarmarc, Carmen was not allowed to go into the airport to use the bathroom but got on the van with no windows. The driver said hello and offered Carmen something to drink and snacks. Her choices were water, juice, soda and milk.

The driver also told her that they were waiting for one more passenger. Agent Debbie said she did not know where they were taking her and didn't know any more details, other than she was safe now. Carmen and the driver waited twenty minutes for the other passage to arrive. The driver introduced himself to her as well and offered her drinks and snacks. Of course he did not give his real name. He instructed the two women not to talk to each other, to keep themselves safe. By the time the van left the airport, it was 1:00a.m., mountain time. They were leaving Salt Lake City airport, headed they didn't know where, but scare and bewildered. The van driver played a recorded tape of soft classical music, once he radioed the contact that he was leaving the airport. Both ladies soon drifted off to sleep and did not wake until the sun was peaking through the sky.

They passed over very mountainous terrain and little view of houses only green pastures and some animals including farm animals, mountain goats, elks and deer, horses very few cars were on the road and the air was brisk. The side of the van where they layed their heads off and on was cold and they would make good use of their pillows and blankets to stay warm, eventhough the driver had on the heat, pockets of cold would whisk across the van as they went through the valleys. After four and half hours of riding and one bathroom break with a early morning breakfast stopping at a truck stop only allowed to get out of the van for the bathroom, the driver ordered breakfast for the two ladies and made them eat in the van. The driver made sure that the ladies understood that it was not his idea to have them not go into the diner to eat, but that it was orders given to him to follow to keep the ladies safe. They looked discussed, but nodded that they understood his instructions and were willing to comply with his request. The ladies did talk a little to each other while the driver was waiting for their breakfast order. Their number one complaint was that they felt dirty and smelly after their flight and the drive and could not wait to take a shower and put on fresh clothes. Each lady had a small carryon bag that was packed by Federal Agents with no connections nor information of where they had come from. In their luggage was minimal items to get them from point A to point B. According to what Carmen had told Agent Debbie that was necessary for her to have for a few days was makeup, jewelry, new underwear, deodorant, razor, soap, hair products (comb and brush), changing clothes, perhaps jeans, t-shirt, bra, night gown, sweater, coat, slips, sneakers, head covering, Tylenol, antacid, and a few other things for her comfort.

Although Carmen had made her request for things, she would not get everything that she requested. Agent Debbie said that the facility that she would be going to would supply other items that she requested. However, Carmen's main request, was that she wanted to go home to Momma Rosa. Of course Agent Debbie said that was out of the question. The other lady was a lot more demanding about what she wanted, she was use to the finer things in life being married to a politician, who had threatened to kill her, because she found out about his mistress, who he had the entire time he was in political office. She didn't have any young kids and her husband would have turned her twenty-two year old son and eighteen year old daughter against her anyway. She had some mental issues and was never close to her kids, but her husband had already planted the seed in them at a young age that their mom was unstable and she had tried to kill herself several times. She felt so alone. Her mother had died when she was only eight years old and therefore her grandmother raised her. She met her husband in college and fell in love with him. They both went to an Ivey League school where he was deemed as most likely to succeed. Her name was Victoria and his name was Walter Sygman. He was a politician when she met him and he was very successful in the field of government in high school as well as in college. She had been passed around by many guys in her high school days and then again in college. Her grandmother had raised her to be prim and proper to act like and conduct herself as a smart beautiful lady. Her strong point was her beauty, she was five foot eight slender, blonde with a million dollar smile and she strudded like a peacock.

Her huband found her irresistible. She had a brother who had died of an overdose at sixteen and felt that it was not fair that he left her with their grandmother and their step- grandfather. At a young age, the step grandfather would come into her bedroom after grandmother had gone to bed pretending to read her a bedtime story and bringing her candy and other gifts, only to molester her. So her self esteem was rather low and she was not all that poplar in high school. Either the girls were jealous of her for being so beautiful having all the boys whistle and "Cat Call" at her and desired a chance to sleep with her are the girls thought that she was just another dumb blonde stuck on herself.

There were times when she did agree to sleep with a few boys for doing her homework. Only one boy that she received help from in her classes did not take advantage of her, but felt sorry for her and helped her with her chemistry and math. John Davis was shorter than her and was also a nerd. But he didn't care about being shorter than her and she didn't care about being taller than him. He was what she needed in order to get through high school and go to an amazing college like Yale. Her flight brought her from Indianapolis, IN her hometown. Her husband had already been kicked out of office for allegedly taking a bribe from a single donor, misappropriation of funds, and slandering his opponent's name during his campaign for State Attorney for the state of Indiana. His luck had run out and he blamed her for his failures. Due to the fact that she knew too much of his political screwups, she was a threat to him as well. Walter's enemies were getting ready to rip her a new one. Walter knew he didn't have a leg to stand on, so he agreed to let her go before things got violent and she would get hurt mentally and physically. Besides, their twenty-six years of marriage had run it's course. The ladies saw the driver retturning to the van with their breakfast, so immediately they stopped talking. Carmen did not have a chance to tell her story, but though it best not to say too much anyway. She didn't know who Venito's family and partners were. The driver had gotten the ladies what they ordered. Victoria had ordered an egg white ommelet with a side of turkey sausage and wheat toast, coffee and orange juice. Carmen wanted two waffles, a side of bacon, sunnyside up eggs, glass of two percent milk and coffee. Once he served the ladies with their breakfast he was ready to go. They had reached their final destination, the driver turned off the main road on to long graveled road to reach a gated compound. At the gate, was a security guard who checked the driver's credentials. Once the guard cleared him and the passengers that he was transporting, the driver was directed to a roundabout near a gated entrants. The guard had placed a call after the clearance and ten minutes later a station wagon pulled up. It was faded and looked like a car out of the 70est. A nun got out and instructed the van driver to move the bags into the trunk of the station wagon. The passengers exited the van and got into the station wagon each lady had a head covering only showing their face to the security guard. The nun instructed both ladies to sit in the back seat and to keep quiet. The nun started the car and continued down the graveled road passed an open field, then a field of trees, the nun then introduced herself and asked their names. Her name was Sister Mary Agnes and she said that they were safe now and could talk and remove their head coverings. Within ten minutes of leaving the van driver, they were at a two story building that formed a U shape and was gated. Sister Mary Agnes went into a courtyard through the opening and gave them instructions for when they left the car. The dawn of a new day had just peaked through the horizon and you could see that they were surrounded by mountains. Very few lights were on at the convent, but enough lighting that allowed them to find their rooms. The room at the end of the hall on the left was Carmen's. Once she opened the door, she could see that she had one window that looked onto the courtyard where they got out of the station wagon. Her room was plain and very poor. She had a desk, with a lamp that was next to her twin bed, with a bible on the desk and a note pad, with a pencil holder with, pencils, ink pens, sissors, a ruler and a manual pencil sharpener. Her curtains at the window matched her bed spread which was a solid brown color. She had a single rug on the floor next to the side of the bed where the desk was, a chair at the desk, was the only other furniture that was in the room. Carmen began to cry as she remembered the spacious room she had at Momma Rosa's house and the even bigger bedroom that she had when her and Venito moved into their apartment in the Bronx. This 10x by 10x room was just horrible according to her standards and smelled like peppermint. She remembered as Sister Mary Agnes was going over the rules and describing the room, she referred to the room as "your CELL". It made it even harder for Carmen to adjust thinking that she was in prison. Overall she knew that she was safe and could learn to make the most of her solitary condition. From a small child she was taught to live a meager life style with little accommodations. So it would not be as hard to go back to where you came from if you have too. Carmen was so tired that she slept for three hours. Because there were no locks on the doors, Sister Mary Agnes knocked on Carmen's door several times before opening the door to check on her. Carmen did not hear knocking at all. So Sister Mary Agnes left her a note and advised her to come to the Mess Hall for lunch when she got up. It was literally two o'clock when Carmen was awake enough to read Sister Mary Agnes message and headed to the single bathroom a few doors down from her Cell. In the bathroom was a closet that had essential items such as wash cloths, towels, soap, lotion, sanitary pads, deodorant, baby powder, shaving cream and razors, shampoo and condition, and many more items necessary for your convenience. It was not uncommon for a new guest to sleep the day away. There was no pressure put on a person the first couple of days. However, the work would began right after the two days to start establishing a new identity and working toward a career if you had a projected time of departure. Not all the guest had to go through such rigorous training, because there was some who would be returned back in to society where they came from or were not threatened with death. However some also, refused to change their identity. Therefore they were released back into society on their on recognosence. This meant that some may relocate to another city, state but keep their identity and can not make the FBI or any agency that put them in Witness Protection responsible for their fate or their family who may accompany them into the program. At the convent, the nuns tried to make the transition from the free world as simple as possible. Most of their meals were nicely proportant and tasteful. There was no junk food there. Although at times, some of the local food pantries in the area would supply them with various snacks to give to the children that were apart of the orphanage that they also ran. In that case the other residence would benefit from the popcorn, candy, chips, soda pop, and many other items. Because the convent was such an asset to the small town many of the large surrounding companies would donate funds to assist with field trips for the children as well as sponsor some of the mentorship for the children to go out to a nice restaurant and shop for clothes, books, toys. It was typical for a lot of this to take place during the Christmas holidays. Popular companies would have a holiday tree with a child's name on an ornament and each employee if they wanted to participate, would select a child's ornament from the tree and would be given a list to buy a gift for that child. Every child would receive something for Christmas, even if their belief was not in favor of the Christian religion, however they would be told it was not a gift for Christmas, but something that they may need or want. The nuns were very skilled in protecting the child's religion preference, if they had one. It was Day three of Carmen new life and she was to report to Sister Mary Agnes Cell. It was where she would meet her everyday for her training. For one week the only person she would communicate with would be Sister Mary Agnes. On the first day of the training she was given a new name. Sister Mary Agnes gave her a list of first names that she could choose from. There were thirty names that she had to pick from. Carmen went down the list and only saw about five names that she would even consider. The first was Cassidy, she said it and tried to visualize her personality with a name like Cassidy and it didn't suit her as well as she thought. Then she skipped to the M's and thought Molina, Megan, Priscilla, Tracy, then back to the M's she said, I like Melia, it had a Greek as well as Spanish meaning. Because Carmen did not want to lose her Mexican/Puerto Rican heritage, she chose this name because it fit her saucey flared life. From that point on Carmen would no longer be called Carmen, but Melia, as a last name, she chose Momma Rosa's maiden name to protect her identity. She chose Momma Rosa's mother's name Lucy short for Lucinda. So her new name was Melia Lucy Ortez. Melia date of birth stayed the same, August 21, 1992, as well as her Social Security number. That was something that was a little more tricky to change. After their first few sessions, Sister Mary Agnes gave Melia an envelope with some pertainent information in it so that she could practice and her new name, by saying it and writing it. Melia every so often would forget to call herself Melia and would say Carmen. At times, she thought I'm never going to get this and why not give it up and move back to New York and take my chances. After convincing herself that she would be better off dead, she received word that Momma Rosa was very sick. It was from Agent Debbie who had indirect contact with her but through a courier that was a reliable source she was able to reach out to Melia. Melia knew that Momma Rosa, even though she was very sick, would not want her to return to New York. So Melia cried for days, not being able to get to her grandmother. After being isolated from the other residents, Melia was given a job teaching some of the children in the orphanage and in Witness Protection. They were elementary school children ranging from first through third grade. She had eleven children and sometimes fourteen. It was because some of the children had special needs and were placed in a separate area depending on their disability. On one particular day, a lady came to pick up Jonathan Tyler Thomas a special needs child. He was a seven years old Autism child. On some days he went to school and other days he spent with a specialist and even with his mom Becky. As he would see his mom coming to pick him up, he would show some emotion but not a lot about going with her. Becky took the time to say hello and ask how did John do in class. Because Melia also specialized in special need children behavior, she was given the task of having him so he could interact with other children his age. As the two ladies talked, John would play with his phone that was specialized for him. It had games, people who talked to him, and other things loaded on to it to keep him occupied. His conversation most times was repetitive. He was not a very good listener and needed to always be paying attention to his phone. His phone was his number one means of communication. If John misplaced or lost his phone, it created a real chaotic situation. He would throw things, scream, take off his clothes and sometimes run away. In addition to John having his phone to keep him focused, he was on several different medications. In addition to being autistic, he suffered from seizurers. Becky was so exicted to talk to someone that understood her child that she wanted to spend more time with her but knew that she was limited in what her communication was with other people there. On another day that Becky came to get John, Melia said that he did not have as good of a day as before. Immediately Becky began to cry. She knew that her mom was the only one that she could talk to about her son and the frustration that she faced raising a child with his disabilities. Melia was putting to good use her education. She was really glad that she had received her Master Degree before she went into the Witness Protection Program. She was told by Sister Mary Agnes that her education would remain the same as before changing her name and she would have the credentials that she had before. She also had training in psychology and relieved some of Becky's concerns and frustration with her son. Becky found Melia's words hopeful and uplifted. The more they talked, Melia found out that Becky and John were also in the Witness Protection program and were presummed dead. Only her mother knew the truth. It was not the intent of the Witness Protection Program to keep anyone in confinement forever, but its necessary to teach them to live a new life. So Melia and Becky met at one of the many classes that are taught for women at the convent. They did yoga on Saturday morning, they took a craft class together. The women grew closer and closer in friendship and shared stories of their pass lives and decided that both of them had been done wrong by the men in their lives that they loved. They thought it's not fair that we should have had to change our lives because of them. There are so many women that have been abused just as we have and don't know how to get out of their situation just as we didn't and couldn't leave on our own. We have got to do something about this to protect women. Melia said, lets put our heads together and come up with a plan to retaliate.

Melia and Becky were eating lunch with some ladies who had been in some of their classes and were enjoying a pleasant conversation about different things and one of the ladies name Constance said she was there in the Witness Protection Program because her ex-husband tried to kill her but ended up killing her boss and her coworker in an explosion that her husband had set off at her job, trying to get her. Thank God she was not at work that morning and that the only people that were there was a stocker and the chief manager of her store. Once the authorities knew who they were looking for, they set out a massive man hunt for Arnold Gerald Mayhem. He was last reported seen headed for Mount Clair Falls, state park. It was a rough mountainous terrain, west of Duluth, MN where Connie was from. She said, you see her ex-husband was suffering from PTSD (Post Traumatic Stress Disorder) and refused to get help. He was honorably dismissed from the Marines and was under a doctor's care. He suffered with severe mental illness and would wake up all times of night thinking he was still in the military battling the enemy. I had to get out of there because I feared for my life, said Connie. Several times, he pulled a gun and even a knife on Connie while having a flash back of being in the Marines in combat. I was scared to death each time and did not know if he would follow through on one of those episodes and actually kill me, Connie said. His job in the military was building bombs, denonate and disarm them. When she filed for divorce and she told the judge her side of the story and that she feared for her life, the judge granted her a divorce from her husband, Arnold based on the fact that he did not show up for the hearing and Connie's witnesses, which was one of her girlfriends who witness him curse her and swearing to kill her as well as a co-worker who saw him at the job holding a gun saying that he was going to kill her, but refused to divorce her and get counseling. Even his mom, Katherine told Connie to leave him as she was crying that she hated the military because of what they did to her son. Connie told the judge that she felt sorry for the families of the people at her sewing and craft store that got killed. The store owner, my boss had four adult children and a girlfriend, the stock worker had a wife who was pregnant with their first child. The store employees had planned a baby shower for him in a month, what a tragedy. The ladies found each others company quite comforting and fulfilling to pass the time away of being in the convent and vowed to keep each other encouraged and hopeful. The ladies were dining another time laughing and having a good time when another lady who was new asked if she could sit with them. Of course the ladies said they welcome anyone who wanted to laugh and have a good time. She was from Abilene, Texas and her name was Barbara Jenkins. Barbara had a very thick southern accent. Needless to say, she had a similar story as the other ladies all were apart of the Witness Protection Program and needed to move on with their lives. So coming together with ladies who were their made for an easier time spent in isolation. Each day proved to be more and more rewarding. As the group of ladies were discussing their situation of being abused or of other women who had been abuse, Melia said that she was abused by her boyfriend who was in a big mob family and she had been threatened with death by him. She really loved him and was really surprise that he would go that far, because she believed that he loved her as well. One of the ladies said that love can be real funny like that. She said love can take over your heart and make you believe and trust that person would never harm you or betray you, especially if he treats you nice. Love is blind said another lady. You forget yourself and others when you are in love. Melia said, he was in too deep with his family business and would not betray them at any cost. He was taught to never go against his family. Now Melia had her note pad ready to start planning their strategy. Connie said that she worked at a large craft and sewing store that was a nationwide chain and she was apart of a group of women who donated to a Women and Children abuse shelter. This group of women were world wide and were very protective of their organization. She could launch a campaign to solicit women to join in retaliation of the abusers. First of all, we must identify who those people are that have really been abused and what crime the abuser committed. Anyway this is a serious matter and have to be handled with the utmost care and concern for women and even children's safety.

After Melia went back to her Cell after the long meeting, she was exhausted and excited. The weather had been threatening rain all day long. Finally about and hour later, the heavens opened up and it began to pour down with fierce winds. The thunder and lightning followed the wind, finally the heavy down pour of rain gushed down the side of the building where Melia was housed and throughout the entire compound. Melia laid across her bed and worked on a flow chart to assign duties to the ladies that were participating in this take down. Also Melia jotted down how to approach this project to keep the people involved with planning this attack identity safe and the perfect plot. She knew that it needed to be approached from a business standpoint and umbrellared underneath another company. We must assign peopled based on their qualifications to do certain task (women of course). Slowly as she listened to the rain she was drifting off to sleep. As she slept, she began to dream of her life with Momma Rosa. How she wished that she was a child again. When her and Momma Rosa would go shopping usually if Momma Rosa got a raise or a bonus. Momma Rosa would let her pick out a few outfits, shoes, toys and jewelry. Melia's earliest memory of this was when she was Carmen and five years old. By this time, her father, Javier had been killed but Momma Rosa did not tell her until she was nine. Melia did not remember him when they use to go to the Prison in Utica, NY. Her father had told Momma Rosa not to bring her there again. Carmen was only three. Javier did not want Carmen to remember him that way. So Carmen never asked Momma Rosa about him and she only saw his picture in the livingroom of their apartment to know how he looked. It was a subject never discussed by her and Momma Rosa. She was taught that a child should stay in a child's place and that is what she did.

They would shop at the Manhattan stores such as Conway, Kmart, Foot Locker, Old Navy, Addias and Macy's on 34th Street was always a treat to shop at. Momma Rosa told Carmen it was an upscale Department store and it always hosted the Thanksgiving Day Parade that they went to a dozen times. The first time Carmen remember going to the parade was when she was five and Momma Rosa had forgot to buy Carmen the heavy gloves to wear. Carmen cried because they got up so early around 6:00a.m. on a holiday and then they had to wait so long for the parade to start and by that time they were freezing as they stood at the corner of 46th Street. The crowd was so thick that people were pushing you toward the boundary of the roped off area known as the parade route. Carmen remember enjoying the large statue of floats like Charlie Brown, Big Bird, the muppets and one year Dora the Explorer. However, as she got older, she could tolerate the cold a little better and looked forward to it everytime there was an opportunity to go. Many of their Saturday shopping trips ended by going to lunch, mostly at a Manhattan diner, sometimes at the cafeteria at Macy's. Most of their outings were on a Saturday or when Carmen was out of school for one reason or another. The outings stopped for a while during the time the bombing on 9/11/01, when the trade centers were destroyed.

On that day, we could not believe what was happening as the world watched the most terrifying event in all of United States history. America was under attacked and many were quite moved. Momma Rosa was terrified to think that she would not see Carmen again. The trains/subways were not working that morning after the attack and Momma Rosa was not going to stay at work knowing that her little girl was in danger and needed her. So Momma Rosa said that after informing her boss that she was leaving to go get her little girl, he told all the employees to just leave to take care of their families. Momma Rosa walked from 36th Street to 96th with panick in her stride, you don't know how fast you can walk, when you are scared and fearful. She reached the Catholic School and felt relieved to see Carmen was safe, eventhough she was crying like most of the children.

The whole city was on high alert that someone purposely bombed their country. Once it was known that there were similar airplane crashes, Pennsylvania, Washington, DC, the Pentagon, New York was the main target. The world was in a state of shock for a longtime and thousands of people were killed. The President Bush, made a statement to assure the American people that this act would not go without pentaties and they would launch action immediately once it was known who was responsible for such a hanious act. Melia woke up from her dream and was startled by a loud clap of thunder that accompanied the lightening. She began to cry wishing that she had Momma Rosa to hold her when she was frightened. O how she longed for New York and the ability to sit around without a care in the world. It was Momma Rosa job to worry about, food, bills, the weather and things that were necessary in life. Periodically Sister Mary Agnes would check on all the residence under her care to make sure they were adjusting to their new life by visiting them in their Cell. At most convents, there is no television in the dorms, but sometimes a radio to listen to music or other times that were going on in the outside world, but it can be quite madding if you were really use to those things. When Sister Mary Agnes visited Melia, she brought her some fresh baked chocolate chip cookies and a cold glass of milk. Melia was glad to see her and offered her the only chair in the room. As they sat and talked about how Melia was adjusting by involving herself in activities with other women and her enjoying teaching the children. Things got quiet for awhile and then Sister Mary Agnes asked Melia if she could share something with her and asked her to keep it to herself. So of course Melia agreed to keep it to herself. So Sister Mary Agnes began by saying that she was not always a nun and it was not one of her desirers or dreams to become a nun. However, she started out at the convent in the Witness Protection Program and decided to make it her permanent home. She use to be a call girl in Reno, Nevada and worked for a pimp who owned most of the call girls in Reno. Well she was given the assignment of playing escort to a politician who was there in Reno for a Republican Regional Convention. It was a kick off for one of the presidential campaigns. She was to host this republican supporter the entire week-end at all times. She started in the prostitute business when she was seventeen and had run away from home in Arkansas. The first night that the gentlemen was in town, he wanted to go to The Atlantis Casino for some gambling and to eat seafood at the top of the world restaurant. He was told how nice it was up on the top floor revolving restaurant and the view was spectacular. So they hopped in a cab and rode over from the Lady Luck Hotel in Reno. Bob my John was not impressed with the table games at Atlantics and was ready for dinner around 7:30p.m. So we took the elevator up to the Top of the World restaurant and placed our order. The atmosphrere and view from the top of the restaurant was breathtaking. You could see the houses lite up in the distant mountaintops as well as the lights from the surrounding casinos and stores. The skyline of Reno was beautiful flashing lights and the faint sounds of vehicles horns blaring and sirens from emergency vehicles rushing about, yet relaxing and romantic. The music being played in the restaurant was different from the music in the casino down below. The music was soft, setting your mind in a romantic fashion, mostly ballards were played. Since Bob was in charge I did not choose what to order, but I left it up to him. He ordered us Margaritas, clam chowder in bread bowls and a combination seafood meal, in large glass for two. We laugh and talked about the weather and where he was from and where I was from and he wanted to know what had I planned to do with my life. Our pimp told us to never be offended by a client asking about our life, but never tell them the entire truth, make them happy and want to stay with you their entire visit. Of course my John had no problem being with me and was okay with spending his entire time with me. Sister Mary Agnes real name was Amber and she was twenty-two when she had to flee for her life. One particular night I was accompaning Bob over to Lake Tahoe, at the Harrah's Hotel and Casino where there was a big party being thrown for republicans and we were going to stay there that night. Every Hotel and Casino wanted to host a party either in Reno or Lake Tahoe, so it seemed. Later that night one of the call girls was being beat up pretty bad by her John. So Bob and some other guys tried to stop him and he pulled a gun on everyone and went to his room without the prostitute. The man was high on drugs and alcohol. It was later found out that she had insulted him by saying she couldn't do anything with a Toddler penis and said he had enough money, why don't he get that thing fixed. The next morning he was dead and no one knew what happened. He was a multimillion dollar supporter and the money he was throwing around at the convention was insane. The word is that he died of a self inflicted gun shot womb and killed himself. Everyone saw him with a gun and knew what he was capable of. Of course, his buddies that accompanied him thought differently that one of the call girls killed him. So they searched for the girl that was with him and she could not be found and they saw me and thought that I knew her whereabouts and even questioned me if I had a hand in this crime. I denied that I had a hand in it as well as I denied knowing where she was. These were very powerful people and they will go to great lengths to cover up the truth. Yes and a great deal of money was missing. The truth of the matter is that our pimp stole the money from the supporter and skipped town. There were all kinds of people looking for us to kill us. So some of us were approached by a private eye, who was hired by some democrates to get dirt on the republican candidates that were running for office. So he got me into the Witness Protection Program here and some of the other girls who wanted protection went other places. I felt like it was God's way of warning me that it was time to give up that type of lifestyle. So that's why I said that I'm never going to go back to that life. Sister Mary Agnes felt close to Melia because of their similar situation and wanted to help her adjust to life at the convent and to prepare her for life once she left the convent. Melia was sitting with the ladies that were planning the plot to take care of their abusers and listening to different ones going on and on about their past life and even their boyfriend and husband. All of a sudden, her mind drifted into another world and started thinks about Venito and their first picnic was at Coney Island during the Fourth of July week-end. The beach was so crowded you could not find a seat, unless you brought your own blanket and chairs. The amusement park was filled with children and even adults acting like children. All you could hear were the voices of people having a good time, inhaling and exhaling the fresh sea air. The smell of food from tacos, to cotton candy and her favorite Hot Dogs. They walked the beach for look like a mile to find enough space to put their basket down on their blanket. The waves were crashing to the shore, while sea gulls swooped down picking up the fragments of spilled food or food that was purposefully given to them. Some of the noise they heard was voices shouting in Spanish and English disagreeing adults, children and even dogs on leashes were barking for attention. On another time Venito took Carmen on her first airplane ride. Her first trip was to Las Vegas and Hawaii. She remember the day they boarded the plane out of JFK in New York, it was about 7:00 p.m. on a Wednesday night. You would have thought that they were going away for their honeymoon. The taxi that took them to the airport was earlier than they thought getting them to the airport. They were in the back seat, kissing and chatting, laughing while fundling each other. Before they knew it, the driver of the taxi said here you are at the terminal for Delta Airlines. The driver took their bags out of the trunk of the taxi and the airport porter immediately loaded them onto a dolly. Venito paid the taxi drive and gave him a large tip. Once through the security, which was a breeze, they went to a bar near their designated departure gate. Carmen got a little tipsy and was laughing continuously like a school girl. They boarded the plane thirty minutes before departure in first class. Venito spared no expense when it came to her. As the airplane taxied down the runway and they were at cruising altitude, the flight attendance began with the drink orders and shortly a menu was given to first classs passengers to select their dinner. Carmen also remembered that Momma Rosa served pasta and sauce on Wednesday and she wanted spaghetti and meat balls. She also wanted a green salad.

For dessert she had Tirumusi. Venito ordered a rib eye steak, with baked potato and green beans. Just like a happy couple, they would feed each other then start giggling again. The entire flight, four and half hours they kept each other entertained by goosing each other, laughing and having stumilating conversations. Carmen laid her head in Venito's lap and took a nap for twenty minutes. Venito also took a nap for about ten minutes. As the airplane was touching down at McCarran Airport in Las Vegas, Carmen looked out of her window and saw an array of bright lights. It was amazing she thought that such a place could be so beautiful she could only think about it being like Hollywood with so many lights or as they call Paris, the "City of Lights" and she was excited to know that she would be exploring that city with the one she loved. Carmen knew that Venito was there on business but would do the best to keep her entertained. The Captain of the plane thanked everyone for flying with Delta and invited the passengers to choose Delta again for their flying pleasure. The couple got into a limo that took them to the Wynn Hotel, where Venito had made reservations once Carmen had said she would accompany him to Las Vegas. The conference he would be attending was very close by at the Convention Center and across the street on Las Vegas Blvd was the Fashion Show Mall, Carmen could walk in the overhead crosswalk to shop. Venito told Carmen that his business associate Mickey would be bringing his wife to hang out with them. Venito told Carmen that Mickey's wife Stephanie was very nice and she was easy to get along with and love to shop. Once they checked in the porter took their luggage up stairs and all Carmen wanted to do was take a hot shower and get into bed. Venito agreed that that's what he wanted too. However, it was only 9:00p.m. in Vegas and he wanted to do some gambling. She agreed that he could go do that while she relaxed. The next morning Venito got up early around 6:00 a.m. the time it was in Vegas, which is three hours before eastern time. He reached over and kissed Carmen while feeling on her and saying they were going to have a good time while in Las Vegas and that was not the only surprise he had for her. Just as Venito said, Stephanie was nice, Carmen met Stephanie the next morning after they had been there. She called Venito and Carmen's room once Venito had left for the convention center. Venito said that he would be there all day and he gave her his American Express card along with two hundred dollars in cash to shop and enjoy her time with Stephanie and that evening the four of them would have dinner together. The ladies first went to breakfast in the hotel, then planned a day of shopping. Both ladies had similar taste in shopping and found that their shopping habits were suitable to each other. After they had shopped as much as they could, a limo picked them up and brought them back across the street "The Strip" to the Wynn. They both agreed to take a nap and then head to the spa and pool. The guys got back from the conference at 5:40 p.m. and needed a short time to rest before getting ready for dinner. Since this was Carmen;s first time in Vegas, Venito hired a limo to drive the four of them around Las Vegas and show Carmen the town. Stephanie had been to Las Vegas a half dozen times, "Hell" her and Mickey had gotten married there and conceived there first child there. So Vegas was not new to them. Carmen could not believe how big the Casinos were. She said, "They are bigger than a lot of the buildings in New York. The limo driver, dropped them off downtown and parked on one of the side streets awaiting a call to pick them back up. It was dark and the laser show that was so famous for downtown Las Vegas was taking place. Carmen was like a little kid, she could not stop staring at the laser show, the side acts that were taking place, such as one man bands, magic acts, dances and a concert in between the Four Queens Casino and the Golden Nuggets. A country western band was performing and couples and individuals were grooving to their music. People were walking around with tall drinks, children with light up toys, big hats and much more was to see in downtown. All the casinos their had signs some said, free play, two for one drinks, win a $1,000,000, and much more. There were souvenir shops stating that they had $1 items and $5.00 clothes and 3 for $10 T-Shirts. Once the tour of down town was over, the limo pick everybody up and continued to show the town. Everywhere they went was crowded with people. The night ended with the couples retiring to their suites, because the guys had one more day of meetings at the convention center. After that meet, Stephanie and Mickey would be catching a Red Eye, and (overnight flight) back to New Orleans to celebrate their youngest of three children's birthday. Venito and Carmen stayed one more night in Vegas before he gave her the news that he was taking her to Hawaii. Again Carmen screamed and jumped up in Venito's lap and hugged him tight while kissing his face and biting his ear and ruffling his hair. Venito moved to Southern California to go to college when he graduated high school for about four months. He told his dad that he wanted to learn how to surf and California was the place to go. So his dad gave him the money and told him to be safe. Sure enough, he learned how to surf and decided that he didn't like California as much as he thought he would. So this time with Carmen he was to go to Hawaii. He nor Carmen had never been there, but Venito wanted to go surfing. They caught an early morning flight from Las Vegas and got to Hawaii around 5:00p.m. pacific time. Two hours earlier than Las Vegas time. They landed at Oahu, Honolulu and got a rental car and headed for Wakiki to their hotel facing the Pacific Ocean. The pace their was a lot slower than New York and the driving was a little less hectic. Once they checked in they headed to a restaurant that was recommended by the conceigne at their hotel. This particular night was Karaoke Night and Carmen talked Venito into singng, however he only agreed if they did a duet. So they sang "Endless Love", which the crowded cheered loudly and told them they did a good job. So they rented a moped and cruise the beach to eat oysters and other local seafood the next several days. All the time they were there, they acted like honeymooners and made love every night. Carmen said to Venito that her life could not get any better than this. Slowly Melia got back to the subject at hand and was sidetracked until Becky said, I want go back to a life of abuse, my life belong to me and no one have a right to take that from me. The plot is that once we post a job online with specific job description and number for that particular job, we need to establish the point of execution. We will do one job at a time attack each and everyone of the abusers all over the world. The umbrella company will be in Corpus Christi. Yeah said, Barbara I can set that up, with a Labor Pool, however, our name will be Day Laborers. Because we are assigning someone who specialize in the job we need done and keep our information confidential. Barbara's friend in Corpus Christi name was Sunni and she owned a profitable temporary service their and Sunni owed her big time. Besides Barbara had been beat up and raped by some illegals that worked for Sunni and also, a lot of criminals that Sunni worked with and ran on the side a smuggling ring and other things. So of course she will be more than ready to help. Becky said before she got married and moved from Rancho Cucamonga, California she worked in the Human Resources Department at an Industrial Plant. Each person had a code for that job and some people had the same job description codes to identify the type of job that was needed to be done. Our mission/slogan is The Punishment Fit The Crime.(TPFTC) Our numbers will be assigned liked Social Security Number, but different, we will use 976 as our prefix followed by eight other digits.

The first job is number 9764228999, one person needed who is an expert, a Computer Analyst, whose speciality is Accessing files, writing programs and deleting data, must be able to debug and encrypt files, and erase traces of data. Our first prospective candidate will be Thomas Bradshaw of Bradshaw, Linden, Ogelbee, LLC a Tax Consulting Firm.

The biggest in San Francisco Bay Area and the top firm in Northern California. Assignment must be completed in two days. At the end of the sabotage, said victim will face criminal charges and sentenced to prison. Mr. Bradshaw is accused of abusing wife by throwing her up against a wall, kicking her in the head and hospitalizing her for severe fatigue, and a broken leg. He has been abusing her for well over eleven years and blame her for having an autistic child. The suspect was having lunch at the Cheesecake Factory located in the Union Square Shopping inside of Macy's on the top floor. The Computer Analyst hired to do the job was able to get access to the Firms database and she completed the task in record time. Job two number 9765998999, two people are needed for this assignment. Home Health Care personnel, who specialize in Mental Illness and/or Alzheimer and dementia. Able to assist with ADL's (Activities of Daily Living). Will abduct COF, Oscar Meyer, of Carlsbad, California, owner, Great Food Plant, who is accused of abusing employees in his food packing plant, refusing to give time off for needed surgeries without pay, making work overtime and giving chickens or other food from warehouses instead of overtime pay, limited vacation days, such as half days, and working them every other week-end as part of their hourly salary, no week-end pay adjustments. Before midnight from a bar he frequent grab him by luring him to your car, after date rape drug has been administered in bar, rohypnol or roofies, will be supplied. Take him to a warehouse on his property blindfolded. Torture him over night, do not allow to eat, sleep. Keep eyes opened by taping eye opened with sticky tape, tie hands and feet to chair, strip victim down to underwear, put him on adult diaper, with tabs.

Prick skin with needle, everytime question is not answered correctly (if he is lying), when questioning him. After torture all night, release him blindfolded off onto sidewalk of the 105 Freeway, droopy diaper still on, with a message written on back that said, (I abuse my employees), soaked in his own urine, no shoes, baby powder all over his face, his right thumb super glued to his mouth and he was crying. As planned Mr. Meyers revenge has been successfully completed and he was spotted by the State of California Highway Patrol and was pick-up by them, he was crying and wondered why anyone would want to do this to him. The Patrol Officer on the scence covered him with a blanket and took him to the nearest hospital, and once he was able to speak clearly, he told the local authority who took his statement, that he was kidnapped, drugged and tortured. He did not know why anyone would want to do this to him. Next job #9767998999, one surgeon needed who specialize in removing a ruptured appendix.

The job The job #9767998999, crime, cut the infant baby sheep out of it's mother, she died, and cut the balls off a male sheep, while on a hunting trip in the Smokey Mountains. Governor Bob (Robert) Jones was currently servicing as Governor of the great state of Georgia. Bob was up for reelection of the state and was into his campaign and needed a get away before things got too crazy. He and three friends decided to take a hunting trip to the Great Smokey Mountains for the week-end. Joseph Peele, Adam Debryia, and Buddy (Scott) Higgins. They packed up the Jeep Rangler of Buddy's and was headed from Atlanta to the four hour trip to the Smokey Mountains where they had rented a cabin in the mountains. Their trip was going to consist of drinking beer, getting high, and telling lies in addition to hunting for deer and fishing. The trip was most enjoyable as they passed small towns, large green trees and pastures of livestock, country stores, farm houses and other drivers that were going from here to there, most not in such a hurry. The four guys had left Atlanta five o'clock a.m. on a Friday morning in order to get a lay out of the hunting area. And get a good nights rest to start the hunt and fishing around 4 a.m. Saturday morning. Bob was excited as well as Joseph to go to the Great Smoking Mountains for an all guys trip, neither one had been on this type of trip before, with just guys. All Joseph had done was work all the time, no time for road trips and dealt with a nagging wife and demanding children. His escape consisted of him going to work, working overtime and going to local sporting events. So this indeed was a treat. Bob had been on a fishing trip before, but it was so long a go, since it was with his dad, before he turned eighteen and it wasn't to the Smokey Mountains. Bob had always lived in Georgia and his dad was also in politics. He was Mayor of Augusta when Bob was only nine years old, but his dad never talked politics with him. However, Bob knew by watching his dad, he wanted to be just like him. So he took student government classes in high school and was even President of his Student Government class. Yes he had a nakk for this type of job. So when he was twenty-seven, he ran for political office. The Mayor of Augusta. Unfortunately he did not win the election. He did not give up, but ran again for the same office a few years later. This time he won, mostly because of the popularity that his father had with the people. They thought Bob was too young and would not give the people what they wanted. So Bob served three terms and then, he campaign for Governor of the State of Georgia and yest he won that as well. The new campaign that he would be applying and running for is for a second term as Governor. The guys told jokes and ate beef jerky as they rode for miles at a time before stopping. There last stop before settling in was for dinner. It was still early and the boys wanted to eat dinner before five o'clock. They teased Joseph saying "didn't your Senior Discount start already", then the guys all laughed It was a joke of course, Joseph was the oldest of the guys, but he was only forty- eight and Crackel Barrel did not honor a discount at that age as being a Senior Citizen. I can ask if they give military discounts said, Joseph. I'm retired and have an active National Guard status. The guys said, naw that okay, just in case we have some supports of Governor Bob, they teased again. It was cold and windy when they arrived at Crackel Barrel Country Store, so the guys put on their big winter jackets along with a head covering and joggled into the restaurant. The wait was only ten minutes, since this is a place for early bird specials for fifty-five and older customers. Once seated three of the four guys ordered coffee and two order ice tea and three of them had water. Because it was Friday and the waitresss Hilly said that Cat Fish was the special for the day. Of course one of the guys said they wanted the fish with hushpuppies, grits, fried green tomatoes and another side of okra and tomatoes. One of the guys wanted meatloaf with mash potatoes, gravy and green beans for one and corn for another. One wanted smothered pork chop, white rice with a side of pinto beans and extra vegetable seasoned peas and carrots. One guy couldn't decided, suddenly he blutred out, that he wanted breakfast. He always like the breakfast at Crackel Barrel and always went there for breakfast. So he ordered the Country Breakfast Sampler. He had all the meats they serve with it, hashbrown casserole, sunny side up eggs, grits, fried apples, biscuits with sausage gravy and an extra helping of bacon. The orders were now complete and Hilly took only ten minutes to bring all of the food back. The guys made jokes and teased with Hilly the entire time they were there. She laugh and teased back with them and made sure that they stayed happy. At the end of the visit, the guys pooled together moneys and handed her a big tip. They made their way to the cabin and then decided to go bar hopping for awhile. None of the guys had brought hard liquor and wanted something to warm their insides before going to bed that night. Their cabin was located a top of Grandfather's mountain and the trip to nearest pub was five miles away once you got to the foot of the mountain. They located "Stone out of your Mind" pub and found a park. It was packed with locals and featured line dancing and a local country western band to entertain the guess. The band consisted of six members, one on drums, one on French horn, two guitar players and two girls with tambourines that sang in addition to one of the guitar players. It was still happy hour, so some of the drinks were two for one before 8 p.m. The guys left about 10 p.m. to go back to the cabin and get some rest before their hunting in the morning. At the crack of dawn the guys were up, Joseph fixing coffee and they ate muffins and beef jerky before heading out to hunt for deer. They were dressed in camoflourge clothing and boots to match. It was quite cool so they each had on a jacket, gloves and head covering. The signs where they could hunt was visible from the road and there were rules posted. Each of the guys had there shot guns and additional bullets to shoot the deer. The cabin had videos in it to tell you how to hunt animals if you have never been hunting or to inform you of the latest rules for hunting. The first site the guys got to to start hunting was about 200 feet into the woods away from their vehicle. They stationed themselves about twenty-five feet, pairing up by twos. The experienced hunters took one of the guys who was not that experienced and they use signals to attract the deer to their area as well as supplied treats that the deer like to eat. About thirty minutes into the hunt, the first deer was spotted and was seeking out the smell of the treat that was laid for it. Sure enough the deer was eating the treat when one of the hunters shot him in the forehead, then the breastbone, killing it instantly. As the morning went on, the hunting was not so good.

They dress the one deer that was killed and attached to the back of Buddy's Jeep. After the hunting was over, they had saw a bait shop at the bottom of Grandfather's mountain, so they went there to buy bait for their fishing trip. The area they went to fish at was a stream five miles from the bait shop. The bait owner had told them that shell crackers were biting and were easy to catch with yellow tails, and bass were also biting, but they needed jigglers or plastic worms to snag them. So the guys took the shop owners advise and were very successful. The caught enough fish to bring back to Atlanta, their 30 foot cooler was packed with fish and deer. Also the bait shop owner was a taxidermy person and agreed to cut, cure and package the deer for traveling. As the guys Saturday came to a close, they decided to stay in for the evening and look at dirty movies and play poker and drink. As they were drinking and laughing, Bob got upset that he did not shoot a deer and wanted to go back out until he got a souvenir. So the guys agreed and though maybe he can shoot a rabbit to satisfy his ego. By this time, all the guys were drunk and two of the four were high on drugs. So Bob said that he saw a farm off of one of the main roads and wanted to see what was there. So Buddy agreed to pull the Jeep over where Bob saw a farm. Maybe he is going to steal a chicken. Bob saw herd of goats grazing and decided that he wanted to kill a goat. Even though one of the guys tried to talk him out of it, Bob insisted that he was not going to kill one. Bob then produced a large hunting knife from his backpack and began chasing a male goat on the other side of the fence. After awhile of the other guys waiting in the Jeep, Bob came back with something in his hand, knife dripping with blood and the thing that he had in his hand was all bloody as well. The guys could not believe what they saw, Bob had killed a male goat and cut his balls out. O My God, said Joseph, what have you done. Bob said, I just wanted you guys to know that I have balls and I'm not afraid to show it. Sunday morning had come and the fellows were kind of quiet. As they gathered their belongings and was heading back to Atlanta, the conversations were few and far in between. Bob couldn't believe what he had done. The guys couldn't believe it either, but they all were drunk and it did not dawn on them until the next morning that Bob had crossed into private property and slaughtered an innocent goat and cut his balls out. Bob was so ashamed of what he had done, but he could not reverse the act. The guys agreed to keep this to themselves, being that Bob was running for reelection as Governor and it did not look good for his supporters not his adversaries to know what he had done. The guys were all good friends and were friends of Bob's and would do what they could to protect him. Once back in Atlanta they only told of the good time that they had and did not bring up the bad stuff. After Bob had won the Governor's race and was reelected that he suffered a ruptured apendence and needed immediate surgery. The specialist that normally take the risk that was invovlved in this dangerous surgery was out of the country and the nearest surgeon was located in New Orleans Dr. Ingrid Gupta. So arrangements had been made to fly her in hours before the surgery was to take place. Dr. Gupta performed the surgery and saved the Governor's life. Through private conversation between some ladies, it was found out that the Governor had castrated a goat and removed his testicles. Killing the goat and performing an act of cruelty on an innocent animal. The abused women group found out about it and decided to make Dr. Gupta the only surgeon capable of performing the procedure. The outcome of the surgery was good, however, the Governor suffered internal bleeding months later, that was unrelated to the surgery. Dr. Gupta had performed Job #9767998999. It was considered complete and the Governor would continue to have continuous internal bleeding over the course of years and would eventually die. After a long hot summer Diane and some of the Plus size ladies at her boutique had meant to her that they felt so ugly and ashamed of their size and wanted to enjoy wearing a swim suit and going to the beach, but the stares that they have gotten in the past made them uncomfortable. Yes and some of her customers stated that they could hear people talking about them and laughing in the background, just walking past them. Shirley one of Diane's faithful customers said her husband left her for a skinny ass blonde who couldn't even spell potato and had body odor that made you want to die. Shirley began to cry and ask why God let me look this way. My mother was big and she had no answer for me and I don't eat that much, so I'm not sure why I can't lose weight. So Diane being the passionate person that she is decided to reach out to some of the ladies that frequent her shop to see if they were willing to come to a Party for plus size women only. Diane said it will be a Pool Party. We will have a DJ, food, drinks and wear whatever swimwear we want. NO SKINNY CHICKS ALLOWED! So several of the ladies agreed and were excited to participate in that kind of activity. Diane began planning the event and told the ladies exactly how much it would cost and that it will be held at a nice apartment complex where she knew the Office Manager. Diane went home and talked to her boyfriend Steve who was in charge of several apartment complexes to see what he could do for the ladies. So he agree to look into it and get back to her about it. Within a few days he said that the Party can take place at the Rio Vista Apartment Complex near Miami Beach. The date was set and the money was paid to Steve to make sure all was well. However, Steve had other plans in mind. The day had come and the ladies were arriving for a Saturday evening of fun and relaxation. The news had been revealed to Diane shortly before the event started that Steve was pulling a trick and had plans of stopping the party. Geiveve was a Federal Agent who was also attending the party and had inside information about Steve plans to disrupt the Party and she would intervene to stop his deception. The women were coming in and music was playing and there was dancing, some were lounging in the chaise loungers with drinks in hand while chit chatting, some in the pool and others at the Tiki bar ordering their drinks while munching on snacks. The DJ was playing "Last Saturday Night" by Katy Perry and the atmosphere was lite. No children, no men except for the DJ and Bartender were present. All of a sudden, Steve appeared, dressed in a short set, with opened toe sandles, shirt opened showing his chocolate oily skin, sun glasses and a smile on his face and told the ladies that they would have to leave and the Property Owners were calling the police to escort them off the premises. What said Diane and other ladies, some of the ladies began to cry, while others gathered around him cursing and shouting you are going to give me my money back, I have been waiting for months for this, no kids, no man, just time to myself, no way this is happening. Diane most aggressively poked him in the chest while cursing and vowing to get even with him.

Suddenly she back him to the pool area and pushed him in. She knew he did not know how to swim. The Federal Agent attending the party allowed him to ask for help several times before jumping in the pool to help him. She yelled, I'll save him, but when she jumped in, she pushed him to the bottom of the pool and sat on him before bringing him up to the surface. Once she pulled him to the outside of the pool, several of the ladies said you should have let him drown. Immediately she began giving him CPR. Two police officers showed one black and one Hispanic while the DJ was still playing the song by Katy Perry, "Last Saturday Night". The officers started dancing with the ladies until the music stopped and began listening to the ladies story of deception. However, there was nothing that the officers could do but insisted that the women leave the property, and hire an attorney to get their money back. The Federal Agent that saved Steve had done her job and told Diane that they could take him to an isolated place, tie him up and each one take turns beating him with an orange tied up in a sock. It would not leave any marks, but would make him sore for a few days. Assignment completed.

Leonard Armstrong was from Macon, GA and left home when he was sixteen to pursue his lifelong dream of becoming a dancer. He was gay before he knew he was gay. When he was growing up in Macon, some kids called him queer, he thought that meant crazy. Leonard grew up with three siblings who paid him no attention. His mom worked all the time and when she wasn't working she was making out with a new boyfriend, who always came to live with them who said that she did not have to work and they would take care of her and the children. Some of her relationships did not last for a year. She would have to find another job that paid her minimum wage and a half ass boss that treated her like shit and even traded money for favors. She often left her kids alone at night while she went bar hopping or pick up a new fellow and slept with him for money. Leonard was often teased by other kids that said he had a black daddy and a white momma. He was never told the truth by his mom why his skin was beige and the rest of the family had cream colored skin. His two brothers left home when he was five. They were fifteen years and seventeen years older than him, so he never really knew them and his young sister was six years younger. All that he knew, is that he like to comb her hair and dress her like a doll. After all she was his pet sister, they didn't have a dog at the time and he was made to watch her while their mother went to the grocery store. He grew up in a trailer park off of Route 16. Most of his friends growing up were girls. He was too sensitive for most boys and he did not play sports. The only guys that he sometimes related to were the nerdy ones and it was mostly to get them to do or help him with his homework. When Leonard was sixteen he told his mother that he was leaving and never coming back. She had a boyfriend that physically, mentally and sexually abused him and he was not going to live in that situation any longer. So one of his friends who was a girl, said that she was moving to Atlanta and going to college there and if he wanted to come and share an apartment with her that he could. Even though he had not graduated from high school, he falsified some paperwork and enrolled himself in adult education school in Atlanta. He worked around his school schedule and saved enough money to go to Performing Arts School in Atlanta. However he was told by one of his professors that he would do real well at the Performing Arts School in New York. So his professor made some calls and sent him on his way. Sure enough not long at being in school he was offered a fill in roll for one of the cast members in an Off Broadway show. He was such a success that he worked his way up to performing on Broadway. Initially as a background performer and then he audition for a major roll and got the dance part. He continued to excel and got a teaching license in dance and was offered a job in Dallas, Texas. Also he had parts that were still being offered to him in New York and decided that if it was convenient that he would take time off from teaching in Dallas and join the traveling Broadway shows for a season. At one of his classes in Dallas he met Bernadette and she took him under her wings to show him how to get around Dallas and learn how to cook. She would invite him over some evenings when her husband wasn't home and they would get along like old girlfriends. One day she didn't expect her husband home from his long distance truck driving job and he came home and wanted to know who he was.

So she say his name was Leonard and that he was teaching her liberal arts classes at the community college. Bernadette introduced her husband to Leonard, she called him Rusty. Rusty didn't take to kindly to her having company, not even other women and now she had a man in the house. He was very angry and ask Leonard to leave. Another day Rusty came home from his long distrance driving and she was not at home and there was no dinner cooked. Once he found out that she was out shopping with Leonard he was angry again, only this time he slapped her across the room for spending time with Leonard. She told Rusty that she was leaving him and that she wasn't coming back. She left him and went home to Tennessee where she had come to Dallas with him, ten years ago. Rusty then asked Leonard to come by his house to get the rest of Bernadette's things because he did not want them there anymore. When Leonard got there Rusty was sitting on the couch drinking a beer and watching basketball on the television. Once Rusty invited him in, he offered him and beer and told him to sit down. Rusty admitted that he missed her and wish she would come back. The more the two of them talked the more Rusty needed someone to cuddle with and Leonard was the only one around. Leonard was scared to comforted him and he was scared not to. So going forward, Rusty felt like this was the only person he trusted besides Bernadette. As time went on, Rusty dependent on him to cook, clean and have an intimate relationship with him. They both maintained their jobs but Leonard moved out of his apartment and into the apartment that Rusty use to share with Bernadette. Findley Leonard broke the news to Bernadette that Rusty had asked him to move in with him. At first she was mad and cursed out Leonard for telling her, but then she was relived saying that she had met someone in Tennessee and wanted to move on with her life as well. She never liked Texas and she missed her mom, her siblings and all her friends. After a year or so Rusty and Leonard started having more and more disagreements. Rusty got very possessive of Leonard and was mad when he had to go to New York or when he took off time to travel with the Broadway shows around the country and oversees. He soon accused Leonard of cheating on him and ruffed him up pretty good. Leonard was approached by some of the case members who got him in an abuse shelter, where he was protected and advised not to return to that abusive relationship. While in the shelter he was put in contact with a woman who said they could prevent Rusty from ever laying a hand on anyone else. So Job #9763118999 was executed. On Rusty's last run from Tallahassee, FL to Baton Rouge, LA his rig was run off the road and jack knifed and slid down an embankment off the Interstate 10 outside of Mobile, AL. He was not killed but his fingers were jammed in the driver side window as he was smoking a cigarette and was flicking the ashes out when the accident happened. Then one of his legs were crushed below the knee while trying to keep the rig from toppling over. Once the paramedics arrived on the scene and he was taken to the hospital, he immediately tried to reach Leonard but without success. He then called Bernadette and asked her to track him down for him. So she did only because her and Leonard had become friends. She contacted the abused shelter and left a message. They did not tell her that he was there but Leonard had contacted her to tell her that she was being beat up on and what shall he do. He didn't want to leave him but he didn't know how much more he could take. So he told her that he was going to an shelter. Given the area they lived in Bernadette contacted the only shelter that was close by. Sure enough Leonard received the message and rushed to be by Rusty's side in Mobile. Leonard had found someone who loved him for him and he knew that Rusty was a decent person when he was not drinking. Leonard was so happy to see Rusty and Rusty him. Rusty wanted to apologize for all the mistreatment that he had inflicted on Leonard and they made up and Leonard told him all that he knew about the abusive shelter operation and how someone set him to say where Rusty would be at a certain time on his truck route.

It was almost summertime in South Florida but the heat had been soaring well into the high 90ties several months before June. Three business partners were planning to get together to celebrate some mile stones in their business venture. Chester, Chet from Boston, Dave from Denver, Colorado who had a home in Miami and Wiley who lived in New York who had a home in West Palm Beach and decided to meet in West Palm Beach, for a few rounds of golf before headed to the Hard Rock Casino in Hollywood, FL. It would be a week-end of celebration of their accomplishing a project that would make them even richer than they already were. Between the three of them, their businesses made them multi billionaires and their gold was to be the richest men in the world and control every part of the globe. They had already made reservations at Hard Rock in a Pent House Suite with three luxurious bedrooms and bathroom combination along with cocktails, maid service and a private bar. It would be the time of their lives, picking up a few girls and getting some much needed sexual services, gambling and ending the week-end attending the Boxing Match at the Hard Rock Stadium in Miami, the last professional fight between Floyd Mayweather and the first fight of Logan Paul. The three men played a couple rounds of Golf in West Palm Beach and the, The Trump International Golf Course. At this golf course they all had quite a few acquaintances and was well known as advivid golfers who frequent this golf course and well as Greenbrier in West Virginia.

The Greenbrier course is where they typically took wives or a girlfriend. It was the most prestigious course in all of North America.

After their golf game, they decided to have lunch at the clubhouse before heading back to Wiley's for some business talk. They each ordered something different, Wiley had buffalo wings with fries a cold glass of beer, Chet had a cold cut club sandwich with potato chips, and a glass of wine and Dave had a cheese steak sandwich with pickles, cold slaw and Ice Tea. Forty-five minutes later that were headed back to Wiley's who lived in a mansion on the intercoastal water way near the Port of Palm Beach. Wiley's wife was not in Palm Beach at the time but was in New York. She was a bridal consultant at one of the top bridal store in New York and was preparing for a major bridal events, besides she needed to keep an eye on their teenage daughter who was seventeen and unrulely at times. Their Manhattan Apartment was located on Fifth Avenue above Lord and Taylor's Department Store. Bridget who was Wiley's wife insisted on living in the Garment District to be close to work and to send their daughter to the Montessori School when she started school at age four. Sarah was now in high school attending the St. Patrick's Catheral Higher Learning School. Several times, Wiley and Bridget had to go to the Police Station to get Sarah out of trouble. One time she was caught in a stolen car with two other girls who she did not realize that the driver had stolen the car, so she got off. Another time she was in the middle of a gang war and was on camera throwing bottles at the police. Because of her father's status in the City, she got off again. At the end of the school year when she was in ninth grade a brawl broke out at the school she is currently attending and again she was caught on camera, hitting a fellow guy student over the head with her textbook. He was not fighting back and was considered an innocent victim. The men sat at an outside patio table with note pads, pens, bottles of water and napkins with peanuts. All sat there by the servant of the kitchen. The guys had a ledger on the table that Wiley produced. It had names, dates, dollar amounts and what the outcome of a service that was performed by that individual listed on the accounting sheet. Each of the men had duplicate ledgers, but because it was Wiley's home, he was able to share what was in his ledger. The men agreed that the ledger was accurate and that they should continue doing business as usual. The real meeting was about their foreign project that was being executed nicely. Over the pass two years a lab in China was funded by their shadow company which they produced a virus that would control the population of the world. The lab was in Ho Chi Ming City a poplar and thriving city after the Vietnam War. America came in after overthrowing the government there and rebuilt a lot of the war torn cities and town. Wiley had married a girl there before the war ended, but she was not listed on any paper that they were married. Anyway Mai Li had maintained the operation and was threatened by Wiley that if she did not cooperate with him in this project that she would be killed. Not just shot, but tortured. Her education that Wiley afforded her gave her access to the lab that produced the deadly virus. The virus administered by her in a rural village to unsuspecting villagers was given to them labeled as a meningitis vaccine. However, it was causing severe breathing problems and in some lead to death. Not all were effected but it was contagious and was transmitted by coughing, dirty hands and salivia. It caused headache, flu like symptoms and sensitivity to light. The quarantine length to be clear of contracting the virus was ten days. There was no cure at the time and it spread rapidly.

The only things that slowed down the virus was to wear mask and wash hands and maintain a six foot distance. Mai Li also monitored the effects of the virus and kept data regarding the strength and the weakness of the virus. Because she had a code system that was only understood by the three men, they were the only ones who knew that the virus was doing what it was designed to do. The next project that the men had created was Christ Church in New Zealand. This lab was operated by MIA's, yes mission in action military personnel, who were supposinly died or were captured behind enemy lines. They were all men that ran the lab in New Zealand, because the three billionaires did not want women working in this lab for fear of them leaking out confidential information. This lab was lab as men only and the reason that they listed that way, was because they said that there were chemicals used that would make the women sterile and that the liability would be great if the women got pregnant and had a deformed baby. This lab housed what they say was the antedote for the menigitus virus that was taking over the world with millions of death and it would stop the virus. Of course the plan had worked to release the antedote to slow down the existing virus. There were many who did not agree to take the antedote for fear of the government taking away their rights to freedom, also the theory was that the antedote contained a chip, which allowed the government to keep track of people's lives. The government was trying to control us some were saying. True enough the billionaires had the virus and the antedote created as their way of bringing the world under their control. Because some countries were not being given the antedote in time, the virus was wiping out some cities killing the whole town. The plan was that over the course of five years, many that took the virus would develop health issues that could not be traced back to the initial virus. The people who decided not to take the antedote would suffer severe complications and would die anyway. So the billionaires were control the entire population with their scheme. The three men had concluded the meeting and were preparing to go to Hard Rock Casino for the week-end. Wiley and Chet would ride together in the limo that Wiley had ordered and meet Dave there. The men arrived at the Hard Rock, Dave first in his Rose Royce, he met the valet attendant who parked his car in a special area for his type of car. The luagage attendant took his bags to a room that was already waiting for his arrival. As a VIP guest (Very Important Person), there was no need to check in, Dave only needed to go to the front desk show his identification and pick up his room key. Dave decided to head to the casino and play a little black jack while waiting for the other two men to arrive. Once the limo driver reached the valet area with Wiley and Chet he opened the car door for them then proceeded to get their luagage out of the trunk of the limo. The two men were greeted by name by the valet attendant and werepointed to the check in desk.

They were informed at that time that Mr. Dave had already checked in. Wiley got on his cell phone and called Dave to find out where he was and Dave told him that he was in the casino near the North Tower playing black jack. So the men met near the elevator in the Guitar Hotel before going to their room. The lobby of the Casino was packed with people checking in and checking out going to eat at the Rise and Shine restaurant the Sushi bar and people going in the gift shops, as they got out of the limo, the cooridor behind the water fall showed a parade of people in the mall areas, laughing smiling and talking very loud. The attire worn was extradinary. Women with leopard dresses and cat suits with one sleeve, stelitos six inches high, Gays mostly guys had on multi color long duster with no shirt and bright colored shoes, some in flip flops, men with T-shirts displaying their favorite sport team, men in fancy suits, people with hats and even dogs on leashes. As the three were entering the room, a sweet smell of fresh cut flowers filled their nostrils. They were roses a multi color bouquet was sitting on the coffee table with a small dish of mints. Over near the kitchen was a fruit bowl with apples, bananas, oranges, grapes, strawberries and keywee. In addition the cash bar was stocked with all kinds of goods, there were potato chips, cheese flavored tortilla chips, wheat crackers with cheese, peanut butter crackers, chocolate candy, the refrigerator had chocolate bun bun ice-cream balls, can sodas, Sprite, Coke, Ginger Ale and Pepsi. The bar had three different wines and a bucket of ice, there was also a case of beer in the refrigerator. The room was stocked with everything that the hotel knew the men ususal like when they came to the Hard Rock Hollywood, FL. Each gentleman went to their room overlooking the large pool area and decided that they would take a twenty minute recess before heading down to the pool area seeking out women to bring back up to the room for the night. Neither of the men were dressed to go into the pool, however once they arrived in the pool area where the DJ was conducting a dance contest and playing poplar loud music. There was not a seat to be found in the area. The men saw one pretty girl after another dressed in two piece bathing suits, some wore thong bikini bottoms, some see through sides on both bottom and top of bikini, others wore one piece bathing suits with just enough of a top covering to hide their nipples. The guys became very excited. Girls of all races looked pretty darn good to them. Several girls were giving them the eye and a nodd becking them their way. The one blonde girl with hair down to her shoulder, nice even tan and a beautiful smile went over to Wiley and asked him did he want to dance and of course he said yes and decided he wanted to ask her to dinner. She had on what appeared as a wet t-shirt undereaneath a see through bra and a thong bikini bottom. Wiley felt his manhood rising to the occasion and knew that she was the one he wanted to spend the night with. The other two men had similar approaches and decided that the girl that they were with was the one they wanted to spend the night with. Before the men decided to get ready for dinner, they asked the girls if they would join them and all three said they would. The three girls were all prostitutes and were hired to entertain these men and set them up to be robbed and be given date rap drugs. After the couples finished eating at the Hibachi Steak Restaurant, the ladies said they needed to go to their room to get some more items before committing to stay with the guys. Once the ladies returned they met the guys in the casino near the north entrance of the hotel. Each of the men were playing a card game and one losing his shirt. The idea one of the others guys said was to win, not lose and the one that was losing at the card game told the other guy go "F" yourself. The guy who was losing decided to play slots for awhile with his woman beside him. All the guys had tickets to go see DJ Khali that night, but did not wait for each other before going. Wiley's girl name was Candice and she was the beautiful blonde who wore a backless red mini dress with a diamond necklace and earrings to match. He was mesmerized by how beautiful she look and thought, he couldn't wait to get her into bed. Dave the guy who was losing at the card table foundly got up from the slot machine to head off to the DJ Khali show, his girl was tall, she matched his 5'9 height. Her dress was a medium blue dress that shimmered every time she walked, her chandelier ears glistered and sparkled with diamonds, she wore ballet flats so that she wouldn't tower over Dave, the perfume she wore tranquilized Dave it was Channel and smelled of lilac and vanilla. He couldn't keep his eyes off her slim figure and long brunette hair that went down her back. They laughed and talked the entire time they were together. She said that she was in college studying to be a lawyer, but wasn't sure if she would make in that field. She had a slight accent, she said that she grew up in Germany and moved to the U.S. when she was eleven with her mother who was trying to get away from persecution by the German Revolt. She never knew her father and was told by her mother that he was killed fighting in Russia. Her name was Nikki, which was not her real name. She was taught not to give her real name when turning tricks. Chet had Sasha who was from Austria and was brought to the U.S. as an infant, by some missionaries and placed her in the Foster Care Program until an Spanish and English couple adopted her at two years old. Her fake job was a Flight Attendant for Jet Blue, but her base airport was Ft. Lauderdale, FL She wore her brown hair up in a French roll with pair shaped earrings. Her neck was draped with a single chain silver necklace with a pair shaped diamond, tear drop. Her dress was puffy around the hips, black in color and fitted around the chest and waist. The sleeveless dress showed her small petite stature. Her perfume was Donna Karan and was soft and frangrant of pomergrated, very tasteful. The show was off the chain as it has been said, DJ Khali was funny and vulgar, but the audience loved his performance. The women enticed the men to go to their room where they were going to have a private party. Once in their room, the women wanted to get in the bath tub and have champagne and wine with strawberries and chocolate. The men were so excited that they requested more fruit from room service, to be brought up to their suite right away.

Within five minute the strawberries had arrived. Candles were lite and the soaking tub was filled half way with warm water and bubbles. Each lady danced in the bedroom where her John was watching as they took off every piece of clothes, while moving to music, and dancing in a sexual manner. Their routine included getting close to the John, but not allowing him to touch them yet, but draped underwear on the John head and start undressing them and moving toward the bath tub filled with flowers, bubbles, while enjoying strawberries and champagne. Each man was so focused on the woman, that they did not even notice that something was slipped into their drink. They became so dizzy and forgot about the naked lady in the bathtub next to him. They each were helped out of the tub and into their bed. The trick, prostitute began questioning him to see how far he was under the influence of the drug. Once the guy fell asleep, each one of them stole his valuables and left the Penthouse without a much as a snicker. Wiley and the other two guys woke up Sunday morning and realized that they had been rob and the girls were no where to be found. Immediately they contacted the casino security to inform them of what had happen and to see if they could check the cameras in the casino to see if they had footage of them leaving the casino. Unfortunately secure were unable to track down accurate footage of the ladies, because they wore a disguise, from the hair to the body shapes. They were phony and they used fake names. Wiley wanted to kick himself because he wore his Rolex watch and a ten carat ring and a gold chain. The value of all that was taken was $45,000.00 in jewelry and money. The other men lost about $7,000.00 and $3,000.00 in cash and merchandise. What a fool they had been to trust those devils with their beautiful smiles and voices. The guys continued with the plans to attend the fight that night and besides Hard Rock had gifted each of their VIP guest tickets to attend and provided transportation to and from the fight. Thank God said, Wiley I had all of my jewelery insured and will probably get most of the cost of that back from the insurance company. Once the men returned home, there was a problem with them going to the bathroom, each one was experiencing some discomfort when that tried to pee. It was a burning sensation that made them scream. Immediately they went to the emergency room to found out what was going on. Each of them were told that it was associated with a date rape drug that had side effects that did not show up until three days of being administered. As they drank the alcohol and the drug mixed together meet up and decided to have a wild party. However it's not contagious and would disappear in another day, provided no more alcohol is consumed during that period of time. This was only half of the job that Day Laborers were completing. The lab in New Zealand was a problem. The lab needed to be destroyed. So a scientist from Australia was contacted. This was a Doctor who specialized in dreaded diseases and ranked in the top ten world as being the best chemist. Since the lab discouraged women scientist and doctors, Dr. Alexander Hazeltine was contacted to dismantle activities at this lab. You see Dr. Hazeltine was born a woman and changed her gender. She represented the best candidate to handle the job. He lived n Melbourne, Australia and was also the closest to the lab. So he boarded a plane for Wellington, New Zealand and took a train to Christ Church to fill in for a scientist that could not make the trip. Dr. Hazeltine's job was to research why the vaccine was not moving as quickly in certain parts of the world. The vaccine was being used on monkeys whose DNA samples were very similar to human DNA and the monkeys were dying from Asia and Indian. However Dr. Hazeltine found the solution to that problem. It was the way that their water was being processed and consumed. He was not ready to report on that matter at that time. Day Laborers hired him to destroy the work of that lab that was linked to the lab in Ho Chi Ming City in China. The research necessary to sabatoge the lab would take six weeks and would require access to various parts of the lab. Dr. Hazeltine had limited clearance for the North Quadrome of the facility, it was the most restricted and needed a higher level of authority to get into that area. Dr. Hazeltine had experience with all types of military and Secret Service knowledge, he served in the United States Military as a computer expert for five years, learning how to write programs, crack codes and creature encryptic messages and set up dummy command jargon. He was also hired by the United State Department of Defense and the Secret Service, and

Home Land Security. However, Dr Hazeltine's passion was in science and he continued his education that he had started after high school at Hawaii State University before moving to the mainland to take a job in Washington D.C. then joining the military to get funds to further his education. Dr. Hazeltine was born in Taiwan and grew up in the Phillipians. After spending time in the U.S. he moved from the United States to Australia, changed his name from Allison to Alexander and changed his gender and married his true love Ginny Burch who he met in the United States. She wanted to return home to Australia to be close to family and friends and to escape all of the bureaucracy associated with the government there. So once Dr. Hazeltine got licensed in Australia he started a research facility to teach college students who were persuing a degree in that field. He decided to take a leave of absence when he received the job offer from Day Laborers to go to New Zealand. Dr. Hazeltine work through the night many times to crack codes and gain access into files that were encryptic. He set up firewalls on his computer to keep hackers from finding out what he was up to. He also set-up cameras with alarm systems around his apartment to detect any intruders. He invented a wand that sweep for bugs in and around his home and car. The wand also detected if a bomb was attached to car or home in the event that someone got curious as to what he was doing.

He did not use the laptop that was provided by the lab to search for wrongdoings by the Exqutex the lab where he worked out of. Dr. Hazeltine was informed before accepting this assignment from Day Laborers that it was dangerous and must proceed with caution trusting to talk to no one about his true assignment there. Before he left home, he told his wife very little of his assignment, only that he was on a special mission for the United States and it would last for about six weeks. She understood the urgency of him trying to do something to stop the virus that was killing millions and was anxious as well to see it come to an end. They had no children only two great danes Handsome and Bruno and a cat named Gracey. The animals kept her busy as well as her full time job at the University of

Melbourne where she taught Psychology. There was always something to do in addition to her spending time with her two sisters Penny married to a lawyer with two adorable boys seven and nine and Abby, short for Abigail a Law Professor at the same college as Ginny. Her parents were world travelers and spent three months at a time in the United States and sometimes Britian. Dr. Hazeltine had finally cracked the code to be able to get into the high security portion of the Laboratory that he was eliminated from. First he was able to see by satellite the makeup of the building and to view the various work stations. His most gruesome discovery was that the lab was run by MIA's who were persummed dead and were no longer in existence. They memory of the men were erased and there was no knowledge on their part of ever having a family or being in the military. They could never go back home. This was the secret that the Billionaires and the military were keeping from the United States citizens. There were make shift labs set up all over the world to create viruses, hause aliening speciments, nuclear bombs, etc.

The United States military, Secret Service and other entities that were apart of building up countries, especially war torn countries and then setting up communities, labs to push their agenda of being the most powerful country in the world. Dr. Hazeltine was the key person to bring down the operation of the three billionaires by destroying there work.

Throughout the world the Day Laborers were slowly bring to a halt, all the destructive abuse brought down on women establishly and even others who face abuse by high powered people. Leonard had told his boyfriend everything, so the authorities began an investigation into Day Laborers in Corpus Christi labor pratices only to find out that they were hiring illegal workers and paying some in cash, not keeping accurate tax reporting information and filing a loss of income for the business two straight years in a row. Sunni and Barbara were found guilty and sentenced to five years propation for running a false business. However Barbara knew that Sunni would eventually get caught and promised to find her a new business, because Barbara had friends who knew judges and lawyers who were working in their behalf. Sunni and Barbara moved to Houston and got real estate licenses and began making more money than ever. Day Laborers became a flourishing business that yielded millions of dollars assets in two years.

It was the third year that South Dallas High School would participate in the annual cheerleading competition.

They were a new school and separated from North Dallas High School which was over crowded and in need of a new school. So they bused the kids within five miles of the Corn Hustlers Highway to the South Dallas High School. As always, the competing schools would travel to Beaumont, TX to participate. Beaumont was about six hours away and required an overnight stay so that all the teams would be there on time and got a chance to participate that day. Only twenty-five teams would be excepted into this competition through out Texas. Some of the criterias for being admitted was applying, registering for the competition, fees needed to be paid by a certain deadlines and age appropriate and a few other things, such as the girl must not be pregnant, no older than nineteen, dressed in school assigned cheerleader attire, not have a suspention status and arrive with team, be enrolled in the current school for first quarter of school year. South Dallas cheerleaders were made up of girls and three boys. There were thirty-five members attending the competition. There were the Junior Varsity team and the Senior Varsity team. There were seven more members who were not able to attend the event and were not apart of the judges decision and they couldn't disqualify the groups for no shows. After everything had been done to prepare the children for departure they all boarded charter buses along with their chaperoning, Head cheerleader coaches and bus driver headed to Beumont. It was early on a Friday morning around 7:00 a.m. that the buses pulled away from the school. Only one stop was made by the bus driver to allow the children to eat and use a bathroom that was not on the bus. The children were hyper and couldn't wait to get there and show their talent. The teams that came from the furthest distance would be the first ones to perform on Saturday morning. The groups had to perform two cheers and stand in a military position and lead by the Team Captians. They would be graded by uniformality, volume and dress code. The judges will select the best out of five teams and the best out of the two teams of five will compete for the the trophy. There were hundreds of students there along with chaperoning and parents who provided their own transportation. Once the first two teams finished that were to show good sportsmanship by clapping for each and every team. The Junior Varsity team from South Dallas High School were the third group to perform. As they were waiting their turn some kids sitting behind them in the beachers began make negative comments in a low voice and touching their hair and throughing things at them like spit balls, paper clips and gum. Of course the behavior disrupted the competition and the team behind the Junior team was disqualified and were sent to a isolated area of the school. Later as the South Dallas High School was leaving the competition some of the boys in attendance as well as a couple of the girls threw red paint on the cheerleaders blue and white uniforms. Security was called and the whole two teams from the opposing team were disqualified.

Sabda Adullah a girl whose family was from India seventeen and Asagar Navado also seventeen had been lab partners in Chemistry at their high school and began to date secretly. The relationship was to be kept quiet at all times. So they agreed to meet at the library to study and have sex. Asagar would get his moms van and drive to the library alone and Sabda's mother and sometimes her father would drive her to the library and drop her off. Both students were honor roll students and had a bright future ahead.

Assagar was taking Paramedic classes at the junior college in his town of Lancing, MI and Sabda was going to be going to college after high school graduation to study Journalism. During their last year of high school Sabda told Asagar that she was pregnant and didn't know what she was going to do and he said that his parents can not know that he was even seeing some one let along know that she was pregnant. He had been telling Sabda that he loved her but this would be so disappointing to his family if they found out. So she said that her parents would not be thrilled either, but she didn't know what to do either. She didn't go any place by herself except the library. So they decided to meet at the library on a Saturday and he was going to take her on a picnic and discuss how they were going to handle the situation. So they met as they always do. He said that he had everything for a romantic picnic in a park near by. She got in the van with him and ducked her head down, thinking no one notice, but his sister thought that she saw someone in the van with him but wasn't sure. Once they reached Avalon Park, ten blocks from the library, the noticed that it was closed. But Asagar knew that it would be closed and said it would be the perfect place for them to have a picnic. He knew she liked hot dogs and she very rarely had them at home so he was going to roast them in the park along with mashmellows. Sabda was so excited to know that Asagar was doing this just for her. They went a few feet into the park a wooded area and he told Sabda to arrange the sticks crisscross while he get the matches and the gas out of the van. So she did what he told her and waited for the fire to get lite. As Asagar was throwing the lighter fluid on the sticks, he threw some on Sabda and told her it was a mistake and apologized. She said it was funny and he continued to squeeze the lighter fluid out onto the sticks. As soon as he felt that the sticks were doused enough, he threw lite matches into the pile of course the fire took off and shot up in the air about two feet, just as quickly as the fire started, he threw a match toward Sabda and said that his hand slipped, but continued dousing her with lighter fluid and more matches. She began to scream, cry and yell for him to put it out, but instead he satuarated her clothes and hair with lighter fluid and kicked her to the ground and walked away, leaving her engulfed in flames, pleading for her life. He ran as fast as he can to the van started it up and took off. It was about two hours before anyone discovered the fire and called for the fire department to attend the fire. The sight became gruesome as they exited the fire truck to see a charded female body lying on the ground completely burned beyond recognition. Asagar's parents were shock of the news that a girl from his school had been burned alive and inquired if he knew her and he denied and said that he didn't know everybody at his school that were from India and insisted that he was there to get an education and not socialize. The authorities were able to identify the burned body when Sabda's family reported her missing. Her father had dropped her off that day at the library and was coming back to get her after 2:00 p.m. but was puzzled when she didn't answer her cell phone and was no where to be seen by the library personnel. However, library cameras saw her come into the library and exit shortly after she got there. They were not able to trace her wereabouts once she disappeared from the cameras surveillance. Asagar's mother inquired about did he see her in the library, because the news said that she was last seen leaving the library and he said that he was buried in his studies and didn't notice anyone coming or going at the library. It took two weeks for it to be discovered that Sabda was pregnant and was at the park with someone, a boyfriend or friend perhaps. The park camera at the entrance captured a brown Town and Country van entering through a blocked baracade. The license plate was not visible enough to see who the van belong too. As television coverage circulated the picture of the van, Asagar's parents relized that it was the family van, by the time they knew that it was Asagar who murdered Sabda, the authorities were already serving a warrant for his arrest. His mother was devastated, yelling why, why and his father had no words, just shook his head in utter disappointment. His younger sister said to him the night of the murder that she saw someone in the van with him and he said you were mistaken and she let the matter go. Asagar was kept in jail and tried as an adult, convicted and sent to prison for life. Due to the continuous abuse and bullying of young people some teenage girls were sick of situations happening to them and decided to start a club, it would be a spin off from Day Laborers and they would call it The Diamond Sister's Club.

www.ingramcontent.com/pod-product-compliance
Lightning Source LLC
Chambersburg PA
CBHW030649190726
48286CB00008B/2735